The Shibboleth Code

Roger Colby

Cover art by Jack Johnson

Twitter: Jack Johnson

ISBN: 0-9896841-6-4
ISBN-13:978-0-9896841-6-3

For my mom whom I'm glad is still with me.

1

Two small gunships, their streamlined hulls scarred and battle-worn, tumbled in the black of space. Loosely joined together by a leaking airlock, they floated in a sea of stars against a backdrop of a purple-hued ionic cloud. Within one of the ships, two unconscious Terrans clung to each other, their life signs very dim, unaware that a massive starship had emerged from a giant wormhole just outside. The colossal dreadnaught blotted out a huge swath of stars, a black diamond with hundreds of jagged spires protruding in all direction, as it closed in on the two minuscule and damaged craft.

Lights on the colossal ship stuttered to life, rippling down the gargantuan hull reflecting across the shiny black surface. Trapezoidal and oblong lights appeared as red and blue orbs or small rectangular pulses of neon purple. The twelve-kilometer-wide ship hung in space, the broken gunships before it like two tiny specks of grey against the growing lights of the greater craft. Out of the mad luminance of the hull came a solid green beam that swallowed the two insect-like gunships. The force of the beam drew vapor from the hull of the smaller ships, and then the tiny craft began to quiver in the green light as another brighter blue-white beam cut through them. The weaker vessels cracked open and splintered into several pieces. What little atmosphere left within coughed out a spray of water vapor that claimed both of the small craft, their detritus bouncing harmlessly off of a faintly shimmering green energy shield.

Hanging in space where the gunships had been were three bipedal creatures, each of them suspended within the safety of the blue-white beam as they floated toward the hulking mountain of a starship. Small chrome orbs formed within the beam near their feet and they were drawn into them, each form vanishing within individual worm-holes.

One second later, two black spheres appeared over individual stasis beds inside the starship's medical bay, their onyx surface reflecting a star field on the other side of each wormhole.

The third wormhole deposited the insectoid creature elsewhere.

Two battered Terrans, a male and female, emerged from the two wobbling spheres in the medical bay. Carried by an energy beam, they floated toward their individual beds, landing softly, caught by an advanced anti-gravity field just before an electric stasis bubble flickered and hummed to surround them in a warm embrace.

Suddenly a crowd of uniformed Terrans burst into the antiseptic room, each carrying various instruments, some of them dragging hover-carts behind them topped with unusual polished-metal tools.

"Get that fluid inducer in them, now!" screamed a platinum-blonde rail of a man, a holographic wrist device feeding him imagery of hearts, lungs and other pulsing organs. "We don't have much time."

"What about the bug creature, Dr. Spurling?" asked one subordinate.

"I will deal with it later!" said the blonde man. "I am under orders to get them stabilized. They are top priority. There will be plenty of time for pet projects later."

The others, a host of twelve Terrans wearing black uniforms with red piping, spread out around the two stasis chambers and went to work. One of them produced a chrome, pistol-shaped device with a spindly needle for a barrel end and plunged it through the stasis field. He grabbed the male human's wrist and jabbed it, only to hear a crunch as the device's business end crumpled.

"We have cybernetics here!"

Dr. Spurling looked up from the holographic readout on his wrist.

"Interesting," he said, one white eyebrow raised. "Did not show up on initial scans. Check for old-form nanotechnology. If he came through the ionic cloud he may not have the latest gifting."

"Affirmative," said the tech. "His system is crawling with them. And they are indeed old form. I've never seen such..."

"Shut your mouth and get to work!" Shouted the Doctor. "Time is short."

Thumping and shouting from the female's table startled the Doctor briefly. The patient was seizing.

"Get that under control, ensign!" he shouted, then turned back to the male patient. "It's a wonder the male hasn't expired by now because of the old firmware. Those nanites were a complete failure, yet we would not be where we are now "

"She is stable, Doctor," said a female tech, her raven hair in a tight bun, her skin pale. "Something...There is something else...in the DNA...the molecular structure..."

"Could it be?" said the Doctor. "We cannot think on this now. We must treat them and then try to sort out their origins later. They survived the ion cloud. Pray to the Divine

Computat they will survive the night."

They worked for some time then, instruments whirring as they sutured, cut, sealed with synth-flesh and argued about the best treatment for the strange nanites coursing through the male.

The Doctor consulted with several of the others before making a decision, and soon they had stabilized their patients. When needed, instruments rose out of the floor as if created out of the metal on which they stood. Soon, less and less of the medical team remained, only the Doctor and two of his closest aides. He stood silent, watching the steady breathing of the two Terrans on the medical beds, and then he left the room, clasping his thin hands behind his back.

He entered a lift, entered a code, and soon emerged in a white room with a plasteel white desk near the wall. He passed through this room into an observation room that looked down on a large chamber where the insectoid alien lay on a stasis bed. Several mechanical arms rose out of the floor and whirred around the bed repairing damaged tissues.

The Doctor considered the events of the past three days. He considered the great fortune, finally managing to locate and retrieve two of the Receptacles. Finding the Receptacles were top priority for the Most High Computat, as they had been stolen long ago by the Shibboleth...a name he loathed to speak much less think about. Soon their quest would be at an end, and once they found the third Receptacle the Most High Computat's perfect order would be put in motion and they would all live forever, understand all things, have access to an infinite mind.

The Doctor folded his arms across his chest and the slightest smile curled one side of his mouth. He would begin the much awaited experiments, and he relished in the idea that they would be inexorably messy.

It was a red letter day.

2

Guillermo's eyes fluttered open, his vision blurred by the haze of slumber, but the darkness of the room dropped onto his face like a smothering hand. The first thing he noticed was cool, clean, antiseptic air and the deep rumble of powerful engines. At the edge of his hearing someone was breathing steadily in and out.

The last memory he could recall was one of sailing through the ion cloud at the edge of the Five Rims, ramming Dervish's bug gunship, and then climbing aboard to stomp the life out of her.

Dervish was most certainly dead.

He then remembered flashes of color, mostly a flurry of activity, of other Terrans working frantically to stabilize his life signs, and then darkness.

He could move, but each movement sent sharp pains through his limbs. He was not restrained, but his wounds ached considerably as his fingers fumbled for his side and his shoulder where he quickly discovered hardened bandages. His fingernails scratched across what felt like hardened nylon. Soon his eyes began to adjust to the faint ambient light and he could see a porthole just beyond the foot of his bed.

He rose, grunting and holding his side, and approached the porthole. Beyond a plasteel window stars streaked by in an endless stream of light like a rushing river of mirrored glass.

The ship was sailing through a wormhole.

"Guillermo?" came a weak voice behind him. He spun around and Mitsuki rose from her own bed, her torso wrapped in a woven bandage beneath a loose fitting gown.

He didn't speak, only rushing to her to take her in his arms. She leaned, her body limp against him as they sat together on her bed in an embrace. It felt good to hold each other in reasonable safety in this cold, sterile room. The uncomfortable darkness seeped out from the far away walls around them but did not seem as forbidding now that they were together. They were lost in each other for a moment, like two solitary bodies orbiting each other in a vacuum.

"I thought you had died," he said, his eyes filling with tears. "Where are we?"

"I don't know," she said. "Last thing I remember was Dervish —"

He stood, began pacing the floor, his wrist against his mouth, his eyes wide.

"She couldn't help herself," Guillermo continued. "She was under the thrall of the Queen and her mind-control device. If only I had known that... but I killed her, Mitsuki. I crulling killed her...couldn't stop myself. Something happened to me back on Fraaz after you went down. I can't explain it. Most of it is a blur...like a dream. I just remember Dervish shooting you, then everything became white-hot, and there was a ringing in my ears like an alarm. Whatever it was I think has to do with the nanites. They...they took over I think. No control."

She reached for him and he plopped down beside her like

a heavy stone. Her arm slid around his shoulder. His metallic hand fell on her knee.

"You need to calm down," she said, her voice even yet faint. "We were being pursued by your...friend...and she tried to kill us both. You are totally justified in any retaliation. Don't grow a conscience because of some prior obligation. She was an assassin."

"But before she went kill-bot she saved my life," he said. "Several times over. The Queen was controlling her using that device of hers...some kind of biomechanical thing."

"You said something...back in the desert...about how the Phaedran Empire quit using the nanites. That they eventually used up their host."

"Yeah," he replied, his eyes staring blankly. "Something about how they were used for war-time, but they caused the soldiers to lose control, consumed their internal structure... the bones and organs."

They sat for a moment, and his hand squeezed her knee. He leaned in for a kiss, but she managed to push him away, a slight smile cracking her dry lips.

"Not so fast," she said with a small laugh. "Right now we need to figure out where we are."

"I don't know," he said. "Can we get back to..."

She stood, ignoring his advances, gave him a wry smile, then grabbed him by the back of the head and planted a kiss on his lips.

After a few returned kisses by Guillermo, she pulled herself away and approached the porthole, looking back over her shoulder with that mischievous grin he loved.

"We are on a ship, no doubt," she said. "But we...did we make it through the ionic cloud? I don't remember much after escaping Fraaz."

"Yeah, yeah," he said, leaning back on the bed on one elbow. "Ionic cloud. The only beings I have seen have been

Terran...I think. I was kind of out of it. Do you think we've found the Phaedran Empire? If so, we should tread cautiously. What we are seeing right now might be an illusion."

She turned to face him, her small hand gripping the edge of the porthole for support.

"Yeah," she said. "Illusion. I'm pretty sure this is all the real thing, Guillermo. At least I feel like it's real. I haven't hurt like this in —"

A metal thunk sounded outside the room and a knife-blade of light separated a far wall where a hingeless opening appeared. A silhouette emerged into the light, and as their eyes adjusted to the glare they saw a figure slide into the room. He was a slender being wearing a snug, black uniform with red piping along the arms and legs. Guillermo dropped to the floor, feet apart, arms folded. Mitsuki moved slowly toward the bed while holding her side. With a wave of the dark figure's hand the center of the room suddenly illuminated, causing both of them to squint at the sudden glare.

"I mean you no harm," said a Terran male, nearly as tall as Guillermo, his platinum hair slicked back, mottled skin stretched over a bony face. He glanced now and then at a wrist band that flashed with holographic lights. His coal-black uniform, however, absorbed all of it. "You nearly didn't make it...we are so glad to have found you."

Guillermo took three steps forward and pointed an accusing finger at the young man.

"That's all great," he said, his left eye twitching. "Where the crull are we?"

Guillermo remembered the stories about the Phaedran Empire, the fact that they had sent a spy to ruin his life, to wipe out the remaining Terrans on the Bug homeworld, all of his friends and family.

"Calm down. You are on the *Victorum*," said the young man, his eyebrows furrowing, but a thin smile cracking his lips. "And I am ship's physician, Dr. Spurling. If you two would get back into bed that would be helpful. You need much rest."

Guillermo didn't comply, stood solid as a piece of durasteel welded to the deck plating.

"I want some answers, Doc. I thought all the Terrans were dead…" He paused, motioning with his hand at the doctor's uniform. "You got a little smudge there on your sleeve, pal."

The Doctor stopped, stared down at a yellowish stain on his sleeve, then began brushing at it with bony fingers. He couldn't quite get it.

"Yeah," Guillermo said. "You just aren't doing anything to it. Could you get some carbonated water, maybe. Make some quick work of that."

The Doctor continued to work at it, let out a puff of frustrated air, then clasped his hands behind his back and glared at Guillermo.

Guillermo's amused grin faded to a scowl.

"I thought I was the last one until a few weeks ago. You are obviously a Phaedran and this is obviously a Phaedran ship. So make with the evil plan explanation and how you want to enslave the Five Rims, how we are captives or whatever, and…you still didn't get that stain, pal."

Dr. Spurling, his platinum blonde hair swept back tight against his skull, cracked a light smile and held up one bony hand.

"Much has changed since our kind were sent through the ion cloud by the rebellion. I am sure you will soon see for yourself that we have parted ways with our former anarchic way of life. If you will return to your bed, someone will explain everything to you when you are ready to accept—"

Guillermo rushed forward, grabbing the doctor by the

wrist. His other hand grabbed a handful of cloth at the front of Spurling's double breasted black uniform just above the stain. The doctor's eyes bulged slightly but he did not resist.

"I want answers, *now*, Doc…whoever you are! I don't trust you or any of the other Phaedrans. Ararchists lie to suit their own means."

Out of the darkness at the edge of the room two metallic chromed skeletons moved into view, nearly noiselessly, shimmering energy shields popping to life around them. They moved so fast they were nearly a blur, suddenly producing long chromed rods sparking blue at the end. Before Guillermo could move he was thumped on the shoulder. All he could manage was a faint "Hey!" before dropping to the floor, his legs suddenly like rubber bands. Mitsuki darted forward only to be struck down, crying out in shock as the crackling electricity flowed from the baton. Guillermo and Mitsuki were fully conscious but paralyzed as the guards scooped them off of the floor and lay them gingerly on their soft beds.

"I regret our actions, Guillermo, but striking an officer triggers security," said Dr. Spurling backing away to the door, one skinny finger manipulating the holographic images that emanated from his wrist. "Please understand that the history of the Five Rims is one of shameful actions by our kind, but we are on the way to making amends, paying penance for our misdeeds. Perhaps after you rest you will be of sound enough mind to reason with us and let us explain our purpose here. I am sorry you had to experience that. It was…necessary, and I trust you are not in any pain. The paralysis will wear off momentarily."

As soon as the automata had finished depositing Guillermo and Mitsuki on their beds, the two skeletal facsimiles strode toward a nearby wall and were absorbed as if falling into a still pool of metal. Otherwise, Guillermo and

Mitsuki were left alone when the Doctor exited the room. The light was extinguished, and then all they could hear was the soft rumble of faster than light travel.

3

Dervish struggled against her bonds, but the pain of her injuries quickly quelled any further movement. She could sense that the chamber in which she was held was devoid of even the faintest odor, her powerful olfactory senses as useless as her compound eyes. The pain that shot through her left eye was nearly unbearable, and her five mandibles clicked and quivered in a strictly autonomic response.

She had somehow survived.

Suddenly she could see some light, a faint but blurry glob of yellowish white at the corner of her range of vision. It appeared to be a window of some kind because two shapes swayed in the middle, blocking the light that backlit their forms. She did not have the anatomy to pick up sounds, but she could feel some vibration through her feet and determined that someone was speaking via a sound system that echoed against the walls.

In the faint light emanating from the distant window she could make out that she had been bound by some type of white bands stretching across her body, holding her limbs in place quite effectively. She could also determine that she was alone except for the shapes moving on the other side of the window.

Something moved toward her. She could feel it stirring the air, the tiny sensing hairs on her legs and arms perceiving the change. She braced herself for more pain, but instead felt a numbness as something was spraying a substance on her wounds. She then felt tugging as a kind of glue was being injected into the cracks in her exoskeleton. She felt pressure as broken carapace was sealed with some kind of shrink-wrap substance that had a foul odor of melting duraplast and antiseptic.

She breathed through her abdomen a clean yet humid air, thick with a moisture that tasted of a chemical nature, and there was a sudden sense memory of her home atmosphere on her world far away. In her mind she saw the tall spires of the Queen's palace, the place from where the vile and traitorous empire had arisen. She remembered that the Queen controlled her armies with an ancient device, a crown of thorny tendrils that subjected all to her will. She had spread out through the Five Rims, conquering each planet with ease due to ancient weapons and ships she had discovered in a secret archaeological dig.

The alliance of the Five Rims planets was broken.

Dervish tensed her limbs with the thought of freeing her people from the control of the despot Queen.

As if they noticed this movement, the metallic arms began to whir, spinning toward her with blurry speed as one of them injected her with a large needle. She fought desperately, but began to drift away to a sudden and uncontrolled slumber.

Her last thought before succumbing to the darkness was that she had to escape, but it faded into the backdrop of quiet oblivion.

4

Guillermo did not sleep.

In the darkness he could hear Mitsuki breathing, but it took a few moments before he could feel his arms and legs. As soon as he could move he was up and pacing the hard metallic floor. He found his clothes folded neatly on a nearby table and quickly dressed out, dropping the strange grey jumpsuit he had been given to the cold floor before donning his heavy boots. He returned to pacing, his boots clanking on the metal in rhythm with his beating heart of rage.

"Could you please return to your bed, sir," came a tinny voice over a speaker far above. "You need to rest if you plan to get better. All of my work will be for naught if you continue to tax yourself."

Guillermo balled up his fists, his body quivering with anger. His eyes suddenly glowed orange.

"I don't care about any of that," he growled. "If I'm your prisoner, then let's get the interrogation over with...or the torture...or whatever the crull you want to do to us."

A metallic squeak sounded then, a rustle of static, and then another voice, a female voice, crackled over the comm.

"This is Commander Deryn Ivory. Everything will be

explained to you, but we need civility to reign. We are in need of your help, actually, and unfortunately due to the propaganda you have been subjected to...probably your entire life... you are not in the right mind to have any kind of meaningful conversation."

"Meaningful conversation," he mocked. "One of your spies royally crulled up my life! And you can call history propaganda all you want but it is what it is. Your group wasn't banished from the Five Rims because you made a few unpopular policies. You were tyrants. Or did you forget all that when you passed through the ion cloud."

Silence.

"Yeah!" Guillermo shouted. "Called you on it, didn't I?! So you just better bring on the interrogation. I've been through a few of them, so I'm an old salt at it."

A sliver of light cut across the room, falling across Mitsuki's bed where she began to stir. A little smile cracked his face as he turned toward the light. The room was suddenly illuminated, causing him to squint his eyes again and rousing Mitsuki out of her bed. A cadre of the chrome, skeletal automatons emerged from the walls like rising from vertical pools of water. They stood evenly spaced around the room, silent drones with blue, glowing eyes. They were unarmed, yet the hair stood up on the back of Guillermo's neck.

"Fancy crulling metal men," Guillermo uttered.

"This penchant for using profanity of the Guajiin is strange," said a dark haired woman entering through the door, her uniform grey, trimmed with red piping, her voice that of the Commander he had just heard. "You have lived too long in the Five Rims, friend. You were able to breach the ion cloud without much trouble, a feat we have not been able to accomplish since the exile."

"So you want to go back and try to reclaim what you left?"

Guillermo sneered. "Well, you better get ready for a surprise, because the Bug queen has probably conquered the whole thing by now. Of course, that was your plan all along I suppose."

"I don't know what you mean by that. We have not sent envoys through the cloud since our arrival here."

"Really," Guillermo said, stepping closer to the Commander, his eyes flashing between her and the automata. "One of your scouts...spies...whatever...was working with the Bug princess to overthrow her mother and also wiped out every last Terran on the Bug world. The Queen has taken Ontocca, is in alliance with the Guajiin, and probably the Fraaz homeworld as well."

Commander Ivory's face was a blank mask except for two steely eyes that studied Guillermo cautiously. Guillermo couldn't tell if he had caught her in a lie or if she was genuinely confused.

"It appears that the Shibboleth have been sowing the seeds of discord in the Five Rims," she said finally. "It is as we thought. But you have a lot to learn about the gaps in history since we left the Five Rims and were forced to survive here in this sector."

Guillermo took two steps forward and the robots shifted their stance in unison, their slender hands at their sides.

"What's with the metal?" Guillermo asked, one thumb jerking over his shoulder. "I mean, your robots aren't really making me feel very safe, if you're going for a good-cop vibe. Besides your kind demeanor, all this heat around us makes this whole situation pretty much the same as the stories I was told."

Commander Ivory stepped closer to him, and now the two were nearly toe to toe. The electric blue eyes of the robots looked on.

"You are a formidable Terran," she said. "I don't know

how to convince you that we have changed, that the Shibboleth is a terrorist entity, or that you are safe here with us. Even though it was my duty to save you from death, to nurse you back to health, I have to calm you down or face scrutiny from my chief security officer whose function is to be a check and balance to my command. These are his drones, and he insisted that they monitor this meeting. Am I now understood?"

Mitsuki, who had been sitting on the edge of her bed, dropped to the floor. She stared at the metal men surrounding them and shrugged, a strange half-smile cracking the corner of her mouth.

"These are new," said Mitsuki walking slowly across the floor toward the wall, reaching out to touch a nearby drone. "Do we get one?"

"Sure," Guillermo said, shooting a smug smile at Mitsuki. "Everybody gets a robot pet in the new order."

Guillermo turned back to the Commander and stared at her.

"Phaedrans, Mitsuki," he said, teeth bared. "These are Phaedrans. Remember what I said about them?"

Mitsuki only shrugged. The automaton she tried to touch stepped calmly away from her and resumed a ready posture.

The uniformed Commander took one step back, raised both hands, palms facing Guillermo.

"You have been told that you were dying, correct?" she said.

Guillermo froze, then stared at the floor, a woven hash-pattern of tiny durasteel cables.

"Am I correct?" asked Ivory again, her patience wearing thin.

"Dying?" whispered Mitsuki, rushing to Guillermo and taking his arm.

"Yes," Guillermo said. "That's what the Ontoccan doctor

told me right before we made that last attack on the shield generator back on Ontocca. I didn't believe it myself and still don't. Something about the nanites eating away at my insides or whatever."

The Commander tilted her head, clasping her hands behind her back.

"Dr. Spurling is the best mind in nanotechnology and biotechnology. In the coming days I hope that you can grow to trust him...trust us. He has isolated the flaw in the program that caused the death of so many shock commandos during the last war, and has managed to correct this error in your physiology. It is all a product of old tech being used for a...well, we will tell you more of our fascination with you later. It was fortunate that he caught the error in time as you were never intended to be experimented upon with such... primitive methods. You shall see that the ways of our ancestors have cursed us to some extent, and you are our hope to change that, but we are working to repay our past transgressions ourselves."

Guillermo cocked his head to the side.

"What do you mean 'never intended'?" he asked. "Do you know something I don't?"

"All in good time, Guillermo," Ivory said. "There are things you don't know about yourselves that we are excited to explain to you. Things that we have waited to share with you. We thought we'd never locate you again. The two of you are from this part of the galaxy, from beyond the ion cloud, and we are eager to help you re-unite with your families."

Mitsuki nudged Guillermo with an elbow.

"Families?" Mitsuki said, her eyes wide. "We have families?"

"Yes," the Commander said. "We are on our way to the colony now. Your mother is still alive, Mitsuki, but unfortunately your father passed some time ago."

Mitsuki backed away, reaching behind her to find the bed and then sink to the floor to sit on the cold metal. She stared at nothing in particular, her mind lost in what she had been told.

Guillermo bristled.

"Don't lie to her," he growled. "If you are lying I will tear this entire ship to —"

One thin hand went up, palm out, Ivory's chin dropping, her silvery eyes staring dead at him.

"I assure you it is not a lie," she said. "And your grandparents are there as well, Guillermo."

Guillermo grit his teeth. He didn't trust them. His mind replayed the killing of the Bug Queen, the slaughter of the Ontoccan delegates, then his fight with the Phaedran agent who had disguised herself as an Aldrassan. He remembered how she had overpowered him easily before disappearing into a personal wormhole. She had planted and detonated the bomb that had destroyed the Terran enclave on the Bug home world, leaving him alone, a terminarch of his own race.

He had then found Mitsuki, and then they were two, and now he stood on a ship, a whole ship full of Terrans.

But something didn't click.

"So I owe you, then?" grunted Guillermo, deciding to play along. "Thanks for the info about my grammy and pop-pops, I guess… and Mitsuki's mom. And by the way thanks for the cure but I feel fine. Not really sure if I was sick in the first place."

"Oh, you were very sick, Guillermo," replied the Commander. "Inferior technology. We were able to augment your nanites with the latest iteration. They should function as normal and give you better control over your abili — "

"When can we leave, then? Or can we leave?"

"You are free to leave at any time, Guillermo," she said, a

vague smile forming. "But we will be arriving at the colony world soon. Your families are eager to meet you. We can provide you with a ship if you so desire, but after we reunited you with your families we hoped that you would stay and help us with our...problem. You may have unique insight..."

Guillermo pushed past her then, his instinct to flee, and he headed for the door.

"Do you have a destination in mind?" asked the Commander with a laugh. "Or are you going to attempt to find your way around a galaxy class cruiser by yourself?"

Two automata appeared behind her and she waved them off. Guillermo mentally remarked at how lightening fast they were.

"I don't know," Guillermo said.

"Perhaps you would like a tour of our ship?" The Commander offered. "Maybe if you are given an all access inspection of *The Victorum* you will change your mind about us. Nothing is off limits...except of course some of the more dangerous areas where the automata do their work."

Guillermo glanced at Mitsuki, then back at the Commander.

"Will our robot guards be in attendance?"

The Commander displayed an attempt at a grin.

"Our guardians are here to protect you," she said, her face growing grave. "We have information that suggests that the Shibboleth have infiltrated our ranks and have designs on both of you. You are important to us, as you are a special breed of Terran. We will discuss this when you are ready, but we thought that you'd want to be reunited with your families first."

"Families?" Mitsuki said, her voice taking on a strange tone. "I have a mother?"

The Commander approached her, helping her to her feet, and Guillermo took a few steps forward.

"Yes, dear," the Commander said softly, reaching up to brush Mitsuki's hair out of her eyes. "Soon you will be reunited with her, and perhaps you will then help us with our greatest achievement."

Mitsuki smiled cautiously, then broke away to approach one of the automata, one curious hand touching its metallic arm. It did not flinch as her small fingers traced a shiny metallic ulna.

"They are designed to keep us all safe," said Commander Ivory. "They pilot all of our fighters, operate many of our lower level functions. Most Terrans hold command positions and leave the guardians to do the more menial tasks of operating this ship. For example, our ship is equipped with the latest in wormhole generating technology, unfortunately to operate the finer functions of the device would be deadly to any organic being. The guardians are an integral part of our forces."

"Nice to know," Guillermo said. "You said something about the Shibboleth?"

Commander Ivory cleared her throat.

"Yes," she said. "We have had some problem with this terrorist organization for some time. They have been very difficult to remove. Each time we find a cell, another cell appears somewhere else. They are a cancer that is eating away at the civility that we have established here, and they are actively planning to erode our plans for ascension."

"Ascension?" Guillermo murmured.

"I know you must have many questions," Ivory offered. "And when you are well enough I will answer all that you have. For now we need you to rest up, eat, and get your strength back. I promise I will help you adjust to your new life with us. We've been waiting on you for some time, and so have your families. You two are special to us in that you were the result of a grand experiment. An experiment we hope will soon come to an end, to give us answers to a problem we have been trying to solve for over a century."

"What do you mean," asked Mitsuki. "For over a century?"

The commander bowed her head as if in reverence.

"The two of you hold the key to our survival."

5

Dervish awoke again, the horrific robotic arms whirring and moving about her. The room was still quite dark, but her injured eye was now working again and she now had full scope of the space around her. Her species had much greater peripheral vision than Terrans, and even though she was not prone to emotional outbursts she came very close to a scream of fear when she saw the mechanical augmentation being melded to the exoskeletal chitin of her arms and legs.

The pain was nearly unbearable, a white-hot searing anguish.

Another chrome plated metal arm extended out of an orb above her, and a needle punctured the hard chitin exoskeleton, injecting her with something that made her a little groggy, but she fought through it and lay still, hoping they wouldn't notice she was still conscious.

She used all of her training to stay alert, to endure the horror that whirred around her. She tried to move, but she was held fast by some kind of energy field, something invisible that only allowed the rise and fall of her abdomen as she took in air. She struggled for a moment, then wondered if her captors could sense her struggling somehow and whether or not they would make her accommodations even more harsh than they were at present.

Another light parted the darkness, a shaft of white from far above her, and she could see two figures staring down at her from behind a thick sheet of plasteel. They wore uniforms that buttoned high on the neck, and one of them, a skinny rail of a Terran with white-blond hair looked on her with piercing blue eyes. He was mouthing something, and she fought through the pain to focus in on his lips.

"The experiment is going well..." and then he turned away, placing a thin hand on the other figure's shoulder next to him as they both moved out of view. The other figure looked strangely familiar, and she thought she saw what looked like large compound eyes.

I will serve no one, she thought. *Never again.*

The drug was beginning to wrestle with her consciousness and she did her best to gain control. She struggled to find a mental foothold, using her cognition keys taught to her by the master of her order, the chief guard of the Queen. She tried to place herself in the past mentally, the chief guard's harsh U'klani rod striking a nerve cluster beneath her thorax to break her concentration.

She had failed the chief guard's instruction miserably in the beginning. Her class derided her often for her weakness, and the master made her remember her failure hour after hour. Sometimes the master would drop in on a training exercise, roust her from slumber, or conspire with the other cadets to lose her in the reed swamp just outside the city. The master, an old Queen's guard who knew of the days of the uprisings and the rebellion against the Phaedran Empire, was more salty than matronly, more cunning than anyone she had ever known.

In the end, after much pain and suffering, she was brought to the realization that the matron master was grooming

Dervish for the role she had come to occupy for so long. Dervish was to take her place as chief guard of the Queen's chambers.

And then she had been assigned to Guillermo.

The Terran was as frustrating as he was crafty. His demeanor and illogical behavior gave her much to despise, but she regretted the actions she had taken against him when under the thrall of the Princess's neuro-bugs. They had caused her to hunt Guillermo down and betray the trust she had built with him, to betray her life debt.

In her culture, to betray a life-debt was an unforgivable sin.

She lay in the silence of the chamber as the shiny robotic arms retracted from her and disappeared into the floor around her. She struggled against the force field one more time, her arms and legs unable to budge even one millimeter. She wondered if she would ever get out of this or if Guillermo was waiting just outside to bolt in and rescue her.

No. No he wasn't. Not after what she had done.

They had tried to kill one another, and both had nearly succeeded.

She struggled against her bonds, felt a minuscule vibration as something loosened, and then she pulled, twisted and struggled against a weakened joint. She calculated that working her arm free might take several hours, but this was not a setback.

The weakened bond felt to her like the warm glow of a winter-ending sunrise and soon she felt the light vibration of a loose bolt falling to the metal floor below.

6

Guillermo and Mitsuki followed Commander Ivory, and after a few rides in elevators and long walks down pristine white corridors, they emerged in a cavernous room filled with large cylindrical pylons that protruded from a ceiling hundreds of meters above them. Automata crawled over every surface, their hands and feet clinging to the metal like chrome plated ants far above. Bolts of blue lightening crackled and jumped between the iron-grey pillars yet didn't seem to disturb the work of the guardians.

"This is the engine room," Ivory explained. "You are looking at the main power source for the *Victorum*, and those pylons over our head are what power the wormhole generators. This is as close as we dare get to them as they are highly radioactive. It is far beyond the technology we once possessed, and our emitters are able to create wormholes small enough to transport a single person or a vessel as large as *The Victorum*. Our computer systems have aided us in enhancing the designs of previous generations, and now we hope to one day escape this sector, find a way to a more hospitable world."

Mitsuki stared, eyes wide at the spectacle far above them.

Guillermo leaned against a railing and tapped it with one metal finger.

"Why are you telling us all this?" he said, crinkling his nose and sniffing the processed air. "I could be a Shibboleth spy for all you know."

Ivory smiled curtly.

"I am taking a risk that worries my chief of security, but I assure you we mean you no harm. We need you to understand that we only desire information about what is on the other side of the ionic cloud. You have lived there your entire life, have been in direct contact with the Shibboleth and seen their meddling in the politics of the Five Rims first hand. You said that they destroyed the Terran colony on the Bug home world, and that you are the only survivor, but you also say that they helped the Queen conquer the Five Rims?"

"Commander," came a voice from above them. "I have locked down reactor seven until I can figure out where the conduits have ruptured..."

Guillermo and Mitsuki looked to the catwalk above them to see a short, stocky woman wearing a red-brown jumpsuit covered in grease, her brown hair disheveled, her eyes covered with opaque welding goggles.

"Guillermo and Mitsuki," said the Commander abruptly. "I'd like to introduce my chief engineer, Clover Adanez, one of the most brilliant technicians I have had the pleasure to work with."

Clover removed her goggles to reveal piercing ice blue eyes that peered out from a face smeared with soot and grime. She did not smile, only looked back and forth at Guillermo and Mitsuki with mouth agape. Guillermo cleared his throat and she blinked a few times.

"G-glad to meet you," said Adanez, yanking a glove off to extend a calloused hand before realizing where she was. "I had heard that we picked up some Terrans from beyond the ionic cloud, but I didn't think I'd get to meet you. Are these two the…"

The Commander gave a nod, and there was a silent communication that neither Mitsuki nor Guillermo understood. After a moment, the stocky engineer spoke.

"Commander we should have that reactor up and running soon," Adanez offered, her voice gravelly and firm. "I don't think it's a malfunction, though. Probably have a spy on board…a saboteur."

The Commander's faced waxed grim, her eyes narrowing slightly. Adanez removed her other glove and tucked them away in her belt. She touched a stud on her belt and jumped over the railing, floating down steadily until she stood beside Guillermo. She reached out and placed a hand on Guillermo's metal arm.

"Nice design," she said. "I suppose this was installed before you came to this side of the ionic cloud? Looks like pre-fall handiwork. I could modify it further if you like."

Guillermo jerked it back from her, rubbing his metal forearm.

"Yeah," he said, his mouth twisting down. "It's the bane of my crulling existence."

She smiled.

"Oh, but it can do so many wondrous things. Have you discovered them all, yet?"

"Can we get on with the tour?" Guillermo asked.

The four of them stood silently for a moment, and when Guillermo glanced back at Adanez she simply pulled out her gloves, put them back on, and then turned away to float to the catwalk above and then disappear into the darkness.

7

The next day Guillermo slowly awoke to find himself in a comfortable bed. He sat up quickly, then noticed Mitsuki who sat comfortably in a spartan chair nearby, her small feet propped up on a white, simple ottoman.

She was smiling.

"I don't think we have anything to worry about, Guillermo," she said to him, her dainty hand holding a silver mug that she brought to her lips. "These Phaedrans or whatever you want to call them seem to be peaceful. The Commander came by earlier and took me on a tour of another part of the ship. They have some pretty amazing tech, stuff that the Five Rims has yet to figure out. Long story short, I didn't feel threatened at all. And I can't wait to meet my mom."

He swung his legs over the side of the bed and crossed to her, taking the cup from her hand and raising it to his face to sniff it.

"What is that?"

"Coffee," she said, her eyes narrowing. "They said it was coffee."

He gave the cup back to her and began pacing the floor at

the foot of his bed.

"I spent the better part of my adult life as a detective, worked undercover, had my fair share of sting operations gone bad. I don't trust these Terrans, Mitsuki. I just don't. Something in my gut is just telling me they aren't who they say they are. I know that they seem trustworthy, and they haven't done anything yet to make me think otherwise, but there's that nagging sensation that the other shoe is going to drop soon."

"Well, they haven't tried to imprison us or kill us so far. As a matter of fact they have patched us up pretty good, are taking us to our families, haven't really kept us from moving about freely, and, well, they've been trying really hard to convince us they aren't lying. I think you need to give them the benefit of the doubt."

"Sure, Mitsuki. Trust them. Every time I trust someone they end up betraying me."

She stood to her feet.

"I haven't."

He stared at her, not responding, his left eyebrow raised slightly.

"Just calm down," Mitsuki offered. "Sit in that chair over there and I can order up something to drink. You want some of this coffee?"

"Something stronger," he said. "Like some Guajiin Ale."

She turned her hand over, holding her wrist near her lips, and Guillermo saw a small band on her arm that lit up when she spoke into it.

"Could Guillermo get some alcohol?"

The wall parted, as Guillermo did not notice a seam for a door, and in came a black uniformed young man carrying a bottle of something with a glass in his other hand. He smiled at Guillermo nervously.

"Sir," said the young man. "I have been instructed to meet

your every need while we sort out your place here."

"Our place?" grunted Guillermo as he approached the young man and snatched the bottle from his hand. Without warning he pulled the metallic plug from it and put it to his lips, chugging down the fermented wine.

At least he thought it was wine. Tasted like wine.

"Will you need this glass, Mr. March?"

Guillermo only stared at the young man and took one more swig straight from the bottle, uttering only a burp in reply.

"Very well, sir," he said, his eyes darting from Mitsuki to Guillermo. "I shall leave you for now. If you need anything, don't hesitate to comm me with the details."

The young cadet turned to go, then looked over his shoulder.

"The Captain will want to see you soon," he offered. "So please do not drink too much of that."

As quickly as he had entered, the young man was gone, the wall closing behind him.

Guillermo sat on the edge of the bed, sloshing the wine around in the bottle.

"You don't think this is all just a ploy to win us over? The Phaedrans conquered the Five Rim worlds with ease, and they weren't deposed easily either. How could a culture of oppression suddenly change their tune in so short a time?"

"I don't know," said Mitsuki, setting her cup on a nearby end-table. "All I know is that we are not in prison, we are free to walk around the ship, and these people seem to be trying to help us…and to return us to our loved ones. I mean, the Commander showed me a hangar where they keep a few transport craft. Said we could take one and go after we meet with our families if we wished, but then started going on and on about how they need us for something. Also that we are the key to defeating the Shibboleth."

Guillermo let out a small chuckle.

"That's just how they lure you in. First they are your friend, then some kind of horrible secret is revealed and you end up running for your life."

"Guillermo," she growled. "This is not one of your old-Earth action dramas. There isn't a smoke monster in the forest!"

The door parted again, and this time a squad of four automata, their skeletal forms reflecting the soft lighting of the room, marched over to stand near the outside wall equidistant from the porthole. They were followed by Commander Ivory and the ship's chief medical officer.

"Is there any way we can talk without these mechanical goons staring over my shoulder?" Guillermo asked, moving to stand between Ivory and Mitsuki.

Ivory's lips grew taught, her eyes flashing around the room as she measured her response.

"I have come to ask you two to breakfast," she said. "Our chef has prepared a grand meal for you, and I expect his cuisine will be to your liking...dishes that would be closer to our species digestive needs. I'm sure the dietary habits of the Bugs were rather..."

"Pretty good, actually," said Guillermo, rocking back and forth on his heels. "Can't complain. I actually miss the stinky chutney they used to serve at that little j'umaa bar in the city. Had to hold your nose when you ate it, but darn fine going down."

The Commander blinked and then glanced at Spurling who only offered a knowing smile.

"I'm sure it will take some time for you to acclimate to the way things have developed since our expulsion from the Five Rims," she said. "In time you will see that the threats we face here are possibly a penance for what we perpetrated during the colonization. Over the meal I hope I can convince you of your importance to our victory over the Shibboleth. I assure you that their destruction is of mutual concern."

Without a word, Guillermo and Mitsuki followed the Commander and Doctor Spurling through the split that formed in the wall. The guardians followed close behind.

As they began the long walk down the corridor, Spurling stopped, his elbows protruding out, his face a grimace as he cocked his head to the side as if listening to a secret voice.

"Commander," he said evenly. "I regret I will not be joining you for the meal. I have pressing matters in the laboratory just now. Perhaps later."

The Commander nodded, and the doctor took a nearby corridor to the left, his gait increasing speed as if he were late for something.

"What got into him?" asked Guillermo, his thumb jerking after the Doctor.

The Commander smiled as she continued walking.

"Oh Doctor Spurling is a very excitable sort. Excellent surgeon and nanobiologist, but his experiments tend to lead him away at the most inopportune times. His bedside manner is very poor, but he is the best surgeon in the fleet."

As Guillermo and Mitsuki followed the Commander to her quarters, the two of them gave each other strange glances, and suddenly Mitsuki's expression became drawn.

8

The darkness enveloped Dervish as she worked free of the last of her bonds. The augmentation that the metallic framework provided gave her more strength than usual even though she was already many times stronger than the average Terran male. She stumbled off of the table where she lay, her advanced olfactory system unable to discern any scent in this antiseptic, cold room.

Suddenly she was bathed in a blinding light and could smell the unmistakable aroma of fear hormone. It caused her to shrink, to fall back against the solitary table, the only furniture in the large, dome-shaped room. She saw movement far above and noticed a Terran male, his platinum blond hair swept back against his grinning skull. He wore a black uniform with red piping, and with a wave of his hand his face covered one wall, projected via hologram so that it appeared to erupt toward her. His mouth began to move and she studied his lips closely as she did not have the physiological capacity to hear sound.

"Welcome, insect," he said. "I have never had the pleasure of studying one of your kind. This is going to be a learning experience for us both. I have augmented your already ample frame with nano-duridium. It has made your carrying capacity ten times that with which you were born...or is it hatched? Many aspects of your physiology are still a mystery to me."

Dervish used a combination of clicks and whirrs of her five sets of mandibles to communicate with Terrans, to mimic their speech in a throaty vibration which took much concentration on her part.

"I will escape this place," she said. "And then I will kill you."

One of the many expressions she understood was that of elation or happiness, and she sensed that the way the Terran's facial muscles contracted over his brow and the way the corners of his mouth twitched that he was indeed expressing this emotion.

"Such brave talk," he said. "I have only seen old history holos which depicted your species as able to mimic Terran speech...with some difficulty it seems...but hearing it for myself is quite extraordinary. Perhaps I shall perform some experiments to see if I can get to the root of how you are able to do that. Your brain is quite complex for such a lower life form."

Before she could read the last word he mouthed, she felt the sting of something hot and then a searing jab at her thorax just at one of the main nerve clusters beneath her more vulnerable abdominal carapace. It nearly brought her to the floor, but she stood her ground, her knees wobbling, refusing to bow before this Terran.

She stared at him, her gaze a laser focus.

"Interesting," he mouthed. "The nerve prod seems to be working as expected. I need to put you through your paces now. Could you please move to that glowing spot on the floor over there?"

As if by magic, a luminescent red circle appeared near the

far wall of the dome and she was compelled to approach it, to get into that circle to stop the pain. It seemed to subside as she approached her assigned goal. Something drove her forward, much like the Queen's controlling arachnids that had burrowed into her brain and caused her to betray her blood-oath to Guillermo.

Guillermo.

She wondered where he was, what had happened to him... to the girl.

Her legs moved almost independently as she staggered toward the glowing red circle. Before she came within thirty meters of it, however, two metallic skeletal automata rose out of the floor as if rising from a still lake. The floor hardened beneath them, and soon they were running toward her. She could see the large face of Dr. Spurling projected before her, a hovering holographic head.

"Do not be distracted," mouthed her captor. "The guardians are only to test you. Do not be afraid of harming them."

Each automata produced a silver baton from somewhere behind them, and as she moved forward the batons grew exponentially until each automata carried a razor sharp spear. She had to slide to the floor as one of them struck at her face with its weapon, and she managed to grab at it and hang on as the metal skeleton pulled her along behind it. She swung a leg around, pulled herself forward, and struck at the crumpling knee joint of her attacker only to feel the hot javelin of the other automata pierce her side.

They were remarkably fast.

She grabbed at the second spear, managing to pull it free and yank the weapon from the second attacker's hand. It gave no expression, only the grinning Terran skull that reflected her own face in jagged detail. She felt another shock of pain as she leaped from the floor and kicked the second automata across the pate. The head cocked back and faced the ceiling only to recoil and lunge back at her, head-butting with enough force to knock her to the cold floor.

"All you have to do is make it to the circle," mouthed the floating head, like a taunting bully leaning down to face her as she lay prone. "The circle is your goal."

She hissed out a blast of air and leapt to her feet, the spear a lethal blur. One of the automata was already reaching toward her, clawing at her carapace with ample metallic fingers. She rocked backward on her heels, springing backward and over it with lithe agility, landing behind it just as the second automata pushed in with a spear. She felt the automata in front of her slump as the spear pierced what had to be a power source, but in seconds the two automata were grabbing at her, the injured one spinning its head to face her.

The floating head appeared again.

"Just make it to the circle and all will be well."

She began to kick, to bite, to claw her way toward the circle then, dragging the two automata with her. They gripped her limbs and pulled at her, their chrome faces grinning, their sharp-toed feet scratching at the floor. Soon she was straining toward the circle, the legs of the two automata sinking into the floor and freezing in place as if they were trapped in the top layer of ice on a frozen pond. She pulled again, tearing their arms free as she stumbled into the circle.

Suddenly she felt a warm sensation, a pleasurable soft rain of joy that ignited what could only be described as bliss. She knew that it was artificial, something awarded to her by her captor, something designed to control her. The head appeared again in front of her, his tightly combed blond hair clinging to his scalp.

"Now wasn't that easy?" He said. "Rest up. Tomorrow we will try another test."

As the lights suddenly switched off, leaving Dervish in

utter darkness, she began to devise a plan to escape.

9

Guillermo scarfed down a mound of potatoes, sopping up a pool of gravy with a scrap of bread with his other hand. He had never tried more traditional Terran food as it was not a luxury Terrans living on the Bug home world could afford. Even though the meal was pleasing to the palate, it still rung of artificiality.

He and Mitsuki had followed the Commander to what she said was her personal quarters where a table had been prepared for them. Two comfortable chairs were welcome pleasures, but the food was much more satisfying. They ate heartily, drank cool glasses of water that tasted like it had been drawn from a well. Both were mildly overwhelmed by the savory aroma of Terran cooking, but again, Guillermo could taste the reconstituted nature of some of it. Not everything was freshly grown.

Two guardians, their imposing skeletal frames reflecting ambient blue lighting, stood silently against the far wall. As Guillermo wolfed down the last of a delicate filet of some kind of meat he eyed the two silent sentinels with suspicion.

"You two on dishes duty?" he asked, clinking the plate with a fork. "'Cause I'm about done here."

No response.

Mitsuki stared at him across the onyx black table top.

"I don't think that's their function," she said.

Guillermo raised a glass.

"Garçon!"

Silence, save the rumble beneath the deck plates of powerful engines.

The doors opened and the automata guards turned their mirror-steel heads in that direction, but then their glowing blue eyes focused back on the three at the table. Through the door came the slender Dr. Spurling. Spurling, his blonde hair slicked tight to his skull, had deep blue eyes that scanned the room methodically. From a black satchel slung around his shoulder he produced a small hand-held device that fit just inside his slender palm.

"I hope the meal was satisfying," said Commander Ivory, her gloved fingers woven together on the table in front of her. "Our mess hall is probably one of the best in the fleet."

Guillermo dropped his fork on his plate, a metallic clang resounding, and leaned back in his chair.

"Fleet?" he asked. "How many of these ships do you have?"

"There are twelve in all," said the Commander. "It has taken much time and effort to build such a force."

"And why do you need so many huge ships?" Guillermo asked. "I mean, if your mission is peace, then you surely don't have anything to worry about."

"As long as the Shibboleth are in this system," the Doctor interjected. "No amount of force will be enough."

Guillermo looked at Mitsuki who only finished the last of her drink.

"And why did you not join us for this...this fine meal, Doc?" Guillermo asked.

The Doctor did not hesitate.

"I had several important experiments running which needed my attention. I am nearing completion of a vaccine to combat a potential plague virus we have encountered on one of the outlying worlds. It is a meticulous process of which I'm not sure you would understand."

The Commander placed a hand flat on the table.

"The Doctor's great-grandfather was instrumental in helping us fight many of the diseases we have encountered since arriving here," she said. "His family have eradicated hundreds of harmful and deadly viruses, and Doctor Spurling has lived up to his family's legacy in the short time I have known him."

Dr. Spurling, his manner not seeming to understand basic social protocol, approached Guillermo, his little device whirring and a series of green lights blinking.

"What the crull is *that* thing?" Guillermo said, pointing with a metallic finger.

"It is a medical reader," said Spurling. "Nothing more. Very harmless. I want to see if the nanites are taking to the new programming."

"I feel fine," Guillermo said, gently pushing the little device away from him. "I don't need your hoo-joo medicine, pal."

Dr. Spurling's pale ears turned a deep shade of red.

"This 'hoo-joo' medicine saved your life, you ungrateful j'agua toad!" shouted the doctor. "I really need you to cooperate if you expect your condition to improve at all! Commander have you informed this man of his importance to our struggle?"

The Commander moved to place a hand between Guillermo and the Doctor. She smiled curtly.

"Doctor Spurling is honor bound to his duty to see you at peak health, Guillermo. You will excuse him if he sometimes forgets his bedside manner. It has been my experience that either a doctor has a great bedside manner or is a great doctor. Nearly never both."

The doctor stepped back, put his device away in the satchel, and offered a short bow.

"Thank you, Commander," he said. "I suppose that idiom is borne out in my demeanor."

The doctor moved to one of the chairs at the table, pulled out a chair and sat without another word. He placed his satchel on the floor then planted his pointy elbows on the table, steepled his fingers in front of him, and then offered a thin smile.

"You will forgive Dr. Spurling," the Commander said, taking her own seat. "He is not used to the rigors of command. His life was one of privilege at the research hospital before I convinced him to join my crew."

"And I am still thinking about it," said Dr. Spurling with a smile, his little yellow teeth very small against pale gums. "I will let you know if I accept soon, I suppose."

Their uncomfortable laughter echoed in the room, but Guillermo and Mitsuki were as solemn as the two guardians who looked on. After a few moments Dr. Spurling cleared his throat.

"Something there is that doesn't love a wall," he said.

Guillermo stared at him, offering a blank expression followed by a short shrug.

"Ancient Earth poet, Guillermo," Spurling offered. "You have built up this wall against your own kind, have been told that we are the enemy for so long, that you have become comfortable in that notion. Some of our kind are of a more violent nature, but after the second coup we managed to follow our better natures. I am sure that once we reunite you with your family you will change your feelings toward us."

Guillermo grinned, picked up his fork, and stabbed a bit of meat. It made a high pitched squeak against the plate.

"Ever heard of T.S. Eliot?" he asked, biting the chunk of meat from his fork and chewing. "And when thyself with silver foot shall pass, among the theories scattered on the grass, take up my good intentions with the rest and then stick them up your —"

"That's ok, Guillermo," Mitsuki interrupted, placing a hand on his arm to silence him. "I'm sure we don't need a history lesson. These people have fed us, taken care of our injuries, and haven't locked us up…which is much better than anyone else we met in the Five Rims."

"I don't know," Guillermo offered as a grim expression melted his smirk. "I can think of several Ontoccans who treated us fairly. They're probably all in camps right about now…if not dead."

Silence reigned once more save for Guillermo's constant chewing. Guillermo's eyes flicked from Dr. Spurling to the Commander, and then he noticed tiny streaks of grey in the Commander's dark hair, streaks that seemed a bit thicker than normal strands of hair.

Are they metal?

Dr. Spurling cleared his throat again to speak, but then Commander Ivory cut him off.

"Your condition was dire when we rescued you from the wreckage of those gunships," she said, her dark eyes focusing in on Guillermo. "Dr. Spurling informed me that your nanites were actually eating away at the rest of your body, desperately trying to repair your injuries while trying to enhance your physiology at the same time."

"I suppose," Guillermo replied, placing his fork on his plate and pushing it away.

"Guillermo…Mitsuki…," she said, her voice trying hard not to sound condescending. "Much has happened since the Phaedran Empire was deposed and forced to sail through the ion cloud. Once our leadership was broken, a new locus of control arose in the form of a peace movement. This movement overcame the Phaedran overlords and reclaimed our more natural inclination to peaceful coexistence. The Five Rim worlds were right to overthrow us, and we took much from them, but the information you lack is that a good majority of the peaceful Terrans who aided in the rebellion decided to go with the Phaedran Empire loyalists in hopes of placidity. After nearly sixty years of sacrifices, the Phaedrans gave in to our methods and a treaty was forged."

"So there are still anarchic Terrans out there somewhere?" Mitsuki asked.

"Yes," added Dr. Spurling. "As I have told you, they call themselves the 'Shibboleth' now, named for some ancient Terran sect that was so secretive that it used a special language to communicate. They have been driven underground, forced to become a terrorist organization that has secret cells everywhere. Now we are tasked with finding these Shibboleth and bringing them to justice."

Guillermo used a fingernail to remove a piece of meat from his teeth.

"Yeah I heard about the Shibboleth. But I heard they were part of a resistance against your empire, your evil empire."

A soft chuckle came from Dr. Spurling. His face grew grave again once he caught Guillermo's steely glance.

"Perhaps the propaganda fed to you by the Five Rim worlders should be expunged," said the doctor, clearing his throat, his lips a thin line. "I have seen first hand what these Shibboleth have done to our outposts here in this sector. I have spent countless hours in the triage units, have seen what their cowardly attacks have done to innocent children. They are a scourge that must be eradicated."

Guillermo's fist pounded the table, rattling the silverware and tipping over his glass of water.

"But I saw one of you," he said, ignoring the water as it

spilled toward Dr. Spurling. "She was a Terran agent...wore a digital cloaking suit that masked her appearance...was an aide to the former Queen the whole time. She killed the Ontoccan diplomats and the queen and then the whole thing was pinned on me. The new queen has been waging a war she says is because of what I supposedly did, something she helped orchestrate, but now she is probably in control of every planet in the Five Rims."

Dr. Spurling grabbed a napkin from the center of the table and began to dutifully head off the spilled water. Guillermo continued to ignore him. Commander Ivory steepled her fingers and leaned back against the high back of her chair.

"You have been through much, Guillermo. We have healed your wounds, corrected the nanite takeover of your physiology, fed and clothed you, taken you on an unrestricted tour of our ship, and you still do not trust me. What must I do to prove our mutual need to work together? You are important to us. You and Mitsuki hold the key to our survival."

Guillermo pushed himself away from the table, his chair tilting back on the two back legs.

"You keep talking about that," he said. "I feel that you need more from us than just information about the Five Rims and the Queen's activities. Explain, please."

"Beyond what the current Bug Queen is doing," offered Dr. Spurling. "There is, as far as our research can tell, pockets of strange matter that interrupt and break down Terran DNA. When our world ships entered this part of the system, they were exposed to this strange matter, forever altering the DNA of many of our species. Even though we are not currently exposed to this phenomenon, having invented scanners that locate the presence of this strange matter, it has generational effects that are quite catastrophic. It requires that we augment our young with nanotechnology, but even that is only a temporary fix. We need to study your DNA in order to determine a cure for the degenerative effects of the exposure."

"Were we exposed to this when we came through the ionic cloud?" asked Mitsuki.

The Doctor turned to her, a faint smile on his thin face.

"As far as we can tell, no," he said. "We took time to scan the both of you as you rested and did not find any trace of strange matter. All Terrans on this side of the ionic cloud carry some trace of strange matter in their DNA, but you two are completely free of it. After we reunite you with your families, we are traveling to Phaedra Prime so that our best minds can examine you, and that is why we have been so anxious for you to stay with us. I hope you understand."

The four of them sat in silence for some time, and Guillermo happened to look at Mitsuki who only stared at her near empty plate of food. She sensed his gaze, and soon they locked eyes. She only twisted her small mouth slightly.

Guillermo spoke slowly.

"I guess I have just been betrayed so many times I can't trust anyone. I'm sorry, Commander. I guess we have to give it time. We can help you with whatever you need. In the mean time, the Terran female who framed me is somewhere on this side of the ionic cloud, I suppose. If she is of the Shibboleth as you claim, then she's been meddling in Five Rims politics for a while."

"It is as we feared," Ivory said. "The Shibboleth are sewing unrest into the Five Rims, using them as a mule for their agenda. These nihilists are only bent on destruction of the Terran race. If they can gain the support of the Bug Queen then they can bring her forces through the ion cloud and our hopes for a peaceful co-existence will be shattered. If there is any hope that you can help us understand the strange matter problem, then possibly it would turn the Shibboleth from their hatred as well, for they are not immune to its effects."

Guillermo folded his arms and nodded at Mitsuki.

"So what do we do about the Queen's armada?" asked Mitsuki. "It won't be long before she comes busting through that ionic cloud."

The commander turned, and when she did Guillermo thought he saw one of the streaks of grey catch the light and glisten.

"We need your help," Ivory said. "You know more about the Five Rims worlds than our intelligence can bring to us. We need to know what kind of forces they have and anything you can tell us about what this Shibboleth woman has done."

"I'll tell you what," Guillermo said. "We tell you what you want to know and you'll follow through with that offer of a ship...after we meet our families and you're done poking around our DNA and all."

Suddenly there was a thundering boom from somewhere far above them and the plates rattled on the table. The two guardians immediately turned and exited through the sliding doors at a clanking full sprint as a loud oscillating klaxon began to scream.

The Commander's face became a brow-furrowing grimace.

"We are under attack," said Commander Ivory rather calmly. "I must attend to the bridge. Coming with me is probably the safest option for now."

The Doctor rose from his chair suddenly.

"I will be in the med-bay in case there are casualties, Commander."

She nodded, and the two Phaedrans hurried toward the door as Guillermo and Mitsuki followed. As they raced down the hallway Guillermo caught up with the Commander as the Doctor sprinted down an adjacent corridor to a waiting lift.

The Shibboleth Code

"Who is attacking you?" Guillermo asked, his voice barely heard over the klaxon as he jogged beside her.

"The Shibboleth have shown their face," she said.

10

The heavy black doors opened with a pneumatic hiss as Guillermo, Mitsuki and the Commander entered the bridge. This ship was much larger than any other ship Guillermo had seen, but he thought the bridge was rather ascetic for such an enormous vessel. The bridge, a box-ended oval room of black metal, was lined with various stations where metallic guardians manipulated green holographic displays so quickly that their hands blurred. In the center of the room stood a holo-table, the neon, three-dimensional image of their vessel hovering half a meter above it and a host of other vessels made of red light hammering it with little arrows of yellow energy.

All of this was secondary in Guillermo's mind next to the imposing, grey haired beast of a man who glared at them from the other side of the holo-table. His bare, thick arms, bearing a skeletal tattoo pattern, were crossed in front of his broad chest. His stony face was tattooed as well with the frightening death-mask of a grinning skull. His grey hair, silver with black streaks, was tied in a tight samurai-style top-knot.

"Commander," said the large man with a surprisingly

raspy voice. "The Shibboleth have begun their assault. We are managing to repel them at present, but I believe this is another elaborate diversion."

"Thank you, Absalom," said the Commander, rotating the image above the table with a wave of her hand. "Have we deployed the countermeasures?"

"Aye, Commander," said Absalom, his ice-blue eyes floating inside black tattooed eyelids. "Am I correct in assuming this deception on the part of the enemy?"

She looked at him then, her green eyes set, and did not speak. Guillermo and Mitsuki came closer, standing near the Commander as she moved a few holographic pages of commands around in front of her. The Commander darted her eyes at them, then back at Absalom.

"This is Guillermo March and Mitsuki..." started Ivory.

Mitsuki stood with both hands resting on the table.

"Just Mitsuki," she said, a wry smile cracking her thin mouth.

"I am trying to convince them to help us," said the Commander.

Absalom did not unfold his arms.

"Security Chief Absalom Liberty," he said absently, then used two large hands to select and pull open an enemy ship hologram, causing it to enlarge.

It looked to Guillermo like a mechanized Fraaz, its bat-like wings spread and its nose the emblem of a screaming Terran skull.

"Their energy signature is getting harder and harder to spot before they de-cloak," said Absalom, his voice an acid-stained purr. "I have Adanez working on it, but she has yet to devise an answer."

"Do not block any resources to her," Ivory said. "Can we use wormholes to deposit them into our hold?"

"They are using an oscillating and transmuting shield

frequency. It's difficult to see beyond it, even with passive sensors, and besides they are too small and moving too fast."

Another pounding from outside and everyone had to grab for something to hold themselves steady. Guillermo noticed that the Security Chief did not, his heavy-booted feet rooted to the deck plating.

The holographic image of Adanez winked into view above the table, her short brown hair a mess, face smudged with grease. Little yellow enemy ships swam through her face.

Mitsuki noticed a strange glimmer of fear in the woman's eyes, something she tried desperately to hide.

"The coolant on aft thruster thirty seven is leaking again, Commander! Give me a couple seconds to lock it down!"

The Commander pounded the table and all the images flickered, the little yellow ships spinning around the Commander's larger ship in a deadly dance.

"Unlock all guardians within range of your position, Adanez!" she shouted. "This I command!"

"I...I live to obey," said Adanez and her image faded, leaving only the swirl of enemy ships swarming like bees.

The Commander spun on her heel, hands behind her back.

"You are right about this being a diversion, Absalom," she barked. "The fighter assault on my ship is futile. They could never breach our shields."

Absalom rested one large hand on the holographic table and he focused his glacier-like gaze on her.

"Commander," he said. "I shall lead a squadron to assault them myself...drive them away from our ship."

She spun back around and Absalom did not react.

"I know it's a diversion," she said. "Chief Engineer Adanez!"

The Engineer's face appeared again, floating in the air in front of Ivory.

"Y...yes, Commander!"

"Give me emergency power," she barked. "We can filter all energy to the shield emitters. The feedback loop will possibly ionize their engines, enough to at least get us out of this Guajiin bee swarm."

"Aye, commander," said Absalom. "Are they attacking that nearby...colony world?"

"Keep your mind on the reactor, Adanez! This I command."

"I... I live to obey."

They felt the ship lurch then, and soon they were breaking away from the smaller fighters and hearing less explosions detonating on the shields.

"It's as before," said Absalom. "I will deploy the sensor buoys. Give us maximum detection aft and stern."

"The colony world?" Guillermo started. "Isn't that where our family —"

Absalom waved his hand for Guillermo to be silent and then gave a signal with his other hand and a guardian against the far wall operated the necessary controls. They could still hear the pounding of enemy fire, but the impacts were becoming less and less frequent. On the holodisplay the little fighters were not able to gain on the larger behemoth, falling back to a distance that the sensor buoys could not detect.

"What is going on?" asked Mitsuki. "Are they attacking the colony?"

The Commander turned to face her. She blinked her green eyes, and Mitsuki could see the steely resolve behind them.

"It appears that again we were held in place while the Shibboleth could mount their real offensive. The fighters hammered us while their larger craft attacked our nearby installation. It has happened before, but we thought we had eliminated all of their larger vessels. I hope I am wrong."

One of the guardians against the far wall raised its hand and uttered a strange, screeching alarm sound. All four of them approached the guardian's station and watched the holo-screen as it shaped the image of a planetary mining installation. Guillermo could see the damaged structures, little holographic fires blazing, pixellated smoke billowing from gaping holes in walls.

And several inert bodies.

The bodies were strewn across the holographic ground like so many moquettes, little holographic forms that unfortunately represented real people. The Commander pounded the console again, this time causing the emitters to flicker and wink out for a few moments before the guardian dialed it in to resume viewing.

"Shut it off," growled Absalom. "Shut it off, guardian."

Absalom placed one skeletal-tattooed hand on the commander's shoulder.

"It is best if you two return to your quarters at this time," he said. "A guardian will take you to…"

"No!" Ivory shouted. "They need to see what these Shibboleth have done. They need to see what we have been cursed with since we made peace with our warlike nature. These rebels must be brought into the light where everyone can see their evil. I only hope their families were spared."

Guillermo and Mitsuki stood quietly as the Commander's green eyes darted back and forth between them, her breathing a steady rasp.

"Come with me," she said. "Absalom, prepare a landing party. Full complement. Let's show these newcomers what we are dealing with. After that they will see what their knowledge of the Five Rims infiltration will do to help our cause."

The Commander turned on her heel, adjusted the tunic on her uniform, and strode toward the lift. Guillermo and Mitsuki felt the cold of the room swallow them as they realized that any family they might meet on the planet below might be already gone.

11

Dervish sat on the floor in the dark near the operating bed. The Terrans had enhanced several of her abilities, namely augmenting her strength through cybernetics, and her vision was now capable of seeing even in pitch darkness. It was a kind of thermal optics coupled with something that would appear in her vision like waves bouncing off of objects around her.

When the light suddenly kicked on she was disoriented just long enough to allow two of the automata to appear on either side of her and grab her wrists. She didn't fight them, as she had been the subject of even more experiments and was biding her time until she found some flaw in their security, some crack in the wall of their resolve.

So far she had found nothing.

Suddenly she felt a new sensation, something alien to her race, and it took her a moment to decipher what was happening. She felt a vibration on either side of her head that at first itched, making her try to raise her hands to scratch at it.

The holographic head appeared again, and this time as he mouthed words in Terran to her she could actually understand what he said without reading his lips.

"Good day," he said, the sound somehow registering in her brain. "Are you able to...hear...me?"

She clicked her mandibles together, releasing a blast of air, then shook her head side to side, the motion more like a vibration.

"I would like to see if the experiment worked without using more invasive methods," he said. "I'd like to get some kind of signal from you as to the effectiveness of the latest procedure. I had to augment your brain with nanotech to get the desired effect, but you should be able to understand me. Those little nanobots should be translating sound to the genetically engineered neurons and then they should be communicating the correct sounds."

At the moment, Dervish felt the introduction of sound to her world like an invasion of her soul. She could read his lips, but the sounds hitting her mind were so strange that she wanted to rip the chitin away from the top of her head and end her life. She fought against the automata, but these were thicker bodied and heavier than previous models she had encountered.

"Please do not struggle," said Dr. Spurling. "We went to considerable trouble to augment your physiology since it is so terribly inferior. The Most High Computat is sending an emissary to oversee the rest of the operation, and I want things to be presentable before he arrives."

"I will make good on my promise, Terran," she hissed. "When I get out of this prison I will eat your throat from your neck."

The hovering face of the doctor smirked.

"Ooh, you are a fighter," he said. "I like that. Couldn't have asked for a better specimen, actually. And the nanites flowing through your system gave us a method of delivery to help us augment you more easily. It is as if they prepped you for surgery. I suppose there is a story for how you have Guillermo's nanites coursing through your system, but that is for another time, I suppose."

Guillermo?

Suddenly there was a noise, an explosion somewhere far away that rocked the ship slightly, and one of the automata slipped its grip on her wrist.

It was the minuscule mistake for which she had waited.

Her powerful leg shot out directly to the side, her hip joints much more limber than that of a Terran, and the automata was ejected across the hard metal floor, its chrome skeleton spraying a shower of sparks as it went. The second automata released a horrific bolt of electricity that nearly caused Dervish to lose consciousness, but years of mental training kept her awake. She used the new freedom of her right hand to grip a cluster of something that looked very vital just below the jaw of the automata.

As she tore it away she discovered that it was indeed very vital.

An alarm sounded and more of the automata began to rise from the floor as if rising from beneath the surface of a pond. But she was ready this time. She lowered into a stance taught to her by an old master, and bounding up and over one of them she raced for the wall. Pain began to ripple through her body again as the floating holographic head just before her out of reach.

"This is not wise," said Spurling. "You will fail as you have always failed. Even though your pain tolerance is quite extraordinary you cannot bear what you are about to experience. Nothing can."

She ignored him then bolted for the nearest wall of the slanted dome and began to climb the sheer surface with her adhesive foot and claw pads. The automata crowded after her, running up the wall in pursuit, their feet and hands clinging to the metal with the hum of magnetic connection.

Something else struck somewhere outside, somewhere far away, and the entire room vibrated.

The automata produced their spears.

She ignored this new development.

Her vision focused on the plasteel window high above and she was sure she would reach it this time.

Suddenly there were bolts of energy blasting out of the walls at her, but she nimbly let go with her feet, hanging on with her hands as she continued higher, narrowly dodging them as she rose. The window came closer, and this time the Doctor was not visible there. She pressed on, and a spear embedded itself in the metal wall just behind her. She grabbed it, using it to swing to the plasteel and use her augmented fist to punch with all of her might at the transparent barrier.

It cracked.

She struck again and again, in rapid succession just as one of the spears pinned her leg to the wall. She ignored the pain, using her deep calming techniques to focus her energy at the window. She jerked her leg free, tearing away flesh and chitin, and struck the window again to slip through a jagged hole and into a white room. She dropped onto a holographic console and then to the hard floor. She glanced at her leg and watched it stitch itself back together almost instantly.

Something suddenly assaulted her, something she had never experienced, and that was the horrific vibration of a sonic alarm that resonated in the small booth. The newfound ability to perceive sound had suddenly become a horrible curse. She clawed for a nearby door, her other hand grasping at her head, the pain punching her brain, causing her to see spots in her vision.

She refused to give up.

Over the cacophony she heard the voice of the doctor.

"This will end if you will go back to the room," he said. "I am nearly done with my study, and after that you may have some freedom."

She struck the door with her fist, waved her hand over the control stud, and shot out into a barren, antiseptic hallway.

"We have cleared the laboratory deck for you," came the voice again. "I am waiting for you at the end of this hallway. Just take the first door you see."

She staggered down the hallway, the loud alarm ringing in her brain, and she scanned the walls for any kind of exit. They were white, smooth, hard as durasteel. At the very end a door slid to the side. As she stumbled through, she saw Dr. Spurling sitting on the other side of a large reflective onyx desk, his fingers steepled in thought, his steely eyes glaring at her, his mouth curled in a sinister grin.

Another blast shook the floor and she nearly fell forward, but the alarm stopped, and she sank to her knees on the hard black floor.

"I am only here to help you find your new purpose, soldier bug," he said, rising arrogantly to his feet and placing his hands on the desk. "Surely you will see that we are on the same side."

As she struggled to stay conscious, a door slid open, and her Queen, the princess who had stolen the throne from her mother after orchestrating her death, one of her mandibles mangled from when Guillermo bit it off, walked calmly through to take the Doctor's seat and stare at her.

<At last we can live in peace with the Terrans> communicated the Queen through pheromones and body language. Then she spoke using her clicking mandibles. "We shall all be free."

12

Guillermo and Mitsuki were given tactical suits and then boarded a drop-ship with a host of other armored Phaedrans. Most of the other Terrans moved about solemnly, their faces drawn, eyes very tired.   When the landing ramp slowly lowered to the dirty, smoking surface of the planet, they found themselves in a burned out mining facility, columns of black smoke still rising in the thin dry air. A column of troops exited behind them. Their armor, resembling black metal rib cages and skull-like helmets, shining in the bright light of a nearby star.

Mitsuki gasped when she saw the bodies, dozens of them strewn around in random chaotic patterns. Guillermo did not see the shapes of able-bodied men, but instead the blackened and still smoking frames of women and children, some of them mere infants clutched in their mother's arms. Mitsuki crouched by one of them, her hand over her mouth and nose. The smell was nearly unbearable.

Someone had strafed this facility multiple times, nearly reducing it to rubble. A nearby technician scanned the area, and Guillermo knew enough about the readout to understand that there were not any life signs in the surrounding leftover husks of what were once dwellings.

He wondered about his grandparents...about Mitsuki's mother.

Commander Ivory was already at the scene barking orders, the stronger automata picking through the wreckage looking for any sign of life. They obeyed her, stating the signature line "we live to obey" which seemed strange to Guillermo. He wondered if this was a hold-over from the old days, the days when the Phaedran Empire was a dominating power, a power that demanded utter loyalty and obedience.

Even unto death.

What he saw on the faces of these Terrans was not the horrific conquerers he was lead to believe the Phaedrans to be. These were people tasked with cleaning up a horrific disaster. They were doing their level best to do their duty, to remove the bodies from the ground and place them on hovering carts, but many of them were fighting extreme emotion as they carefully and respectfully handled the dead. Their faces were masks of compassion, of disbelief and despair, not of tyranny and hatred. These Terrans were expressing remorse.

Guillermo tapped Mitsuki's shoulder and she rose. She followed him as he approached the small crowd of officers encircling Commander Ivory. She manipulated a hologram floating above her wrist, coordinating the clean-up effort, and then made cold eye-contact with Mitsuki and Guillermo as she gave the last of the orders to her subordinates.

"What can we do to help?" asked Mitsuki finally. "Is there anything? Where is my mother?"

Ivory set her mouth, pushed the holographic images into her wrist, and then placed a gloved hand on Mitsuki's shoulder.

"We have not located her yet, haven't found any survivors," she said. "Just when we think we have arrested or destroyed the rebels they pop up elsewhere. This was a mining colony, and this crater you are standing in used to be a school. Their tactics are vicious and often costly, but today they have truly gone beyond the pale. Even though all of my experience with them has been violent and horrific, I refuse to believe that they will never be redeemed. Perhaps if we can learn from your DNA the cure for the strange matter blight we can bring an end to this conflict."

Ivory looked beyond them at the crew who were working to gingerly place a cluster of blackened children on a hover skiff. Her eyes began to water, and the tough exterior melted, transforming this iron-skinned commander into a compassionate woman, possibly a mother.

"Do either of you have children?" she asked.

"No," Guillermo said. "My wife...Meagan. The organic that permeated the ecosystem on the bug world had made us both sterile. She died while I was on assignment."

Mitsuki put an arm around Guillermo's waist.

"I have two boys," said Ivory. "Nine and seven. They live on Phaedra Prime with their aunt."

She looked at Guillermo, seeming to look through him.

"I... The miners had a very good education system here. Teachers were assigned a charge of children from age five, and would educate them and be a mentor for them their entire lives as a student. It was a close-knit community."

She placed one hand on a nearby hover-cart, seemingly more for support than a casual gesture, and scanned the wreckage with red-rimmed eyes.

"The Shibboleth have been hitting our outlying colonies for some time now, working their way inward toward Phaedra Prime. In the beginning of their movement they acted in smaller ways, sabotaging the food supply, destroying fields of grain on our farming worlds, but these past few decades they have been more systematic. We had to carve out a place in this sector after the war with blood and sweat, after the coup that gave us back our humanity. But the Shibboleth were always there in our ranks, whittling away at our morale, sewing seeds of anarchy. Many of the worlds in this sector have been terraformed to suit our needs, but we had to spend a good fifty years on board those ailing world-ships before any planet was safe for us. The Shibboleth were there at every turn, each supposed accident that set us back in progress to terraform turning out to be their early attempts at destroying our fragile peace."

"What do they want?" Mitsuki asked.

"The core of their beliefs, as far as we can understand, is that they want the Terran race to die. It is a nihilistic drive that causes them to seek to disrupt and destroy. They believe that the strange matter that dwindles our race is a curse from a higher power. According to them we deserved the exile from the Five Rims. We understand this...accept it...and have tried to eek out a life for ourselves here on the other side of the ionic cloud even with the blight a constant threat, but the Shibboleth only desire death."

"So what brought about the second coup?" Guillermo said, his arms folding across his chest.

"It took much time but mostly incredible hardship. Our misfortune drove us to peace. Once through the ionic cloud, a group of us realized our horrible wrong and rose up against the Phaedran Overlords. We revolted, much with the aid of the large cadre of super-soldiers who had been re-programmed by our own revolutionaries. Absalom Liberty is one of those near immortal soldiers. Unfortunately, there was no way to return from our exile, and due to our hubris in the past toward the Five Rims we vowed that we would never return. Cut our losses. Try to build a life in this sector without the need for war and for the domination of another species. But the Shibboleth have always been there...and they have decreed a death sentence for us all."

A grim looking soldier approached them, his armor in the pattern of a human skeleton, the skull-like face shield raised cap-a-pate. The young eyes contrasted strangely with his dour expression.

"Commander," he said, saluting by pounding one fist on his chest. "We have discovered some survivors, but they are trapped beneath a heap of rubble."

Ivory's eyebrows furrowed and she bore her teeth.

"Get every able bodied soldier on it, corporal," she shouted. "Wormhole down some guardians as well. We will need their strength to move the debris safely."

"Anything we can to do help?" asked Guillermo, wondering if any of the survivors could be his family. Mitsuki only held on to his arm.

She ignored them both, rushing away with two other armored soldiers, their heavy metallic boots clomping on the hard ground.

Guillermo looked at Mitsuki and her expression was all he needed to understand her. They jogged after the group of soldiers to a enormous pile of debris that lay scattered at the base of a desiccated building. Small wisps of smoke rose out from between the chunks of permacrete, and as they arrived several guardians were appearing out of silvery orbs as if they were angels descending from heaven...large skeletal angels with shining chrome bodies.

The guardians went to work tearing away at the rubble, lifting huge chunks of permacrete out of the way, digging down to the base of the building with a speed that defied logic. Guillermo squinted his eyes, but Mitsuki spoke his mind before he could utter a syllable.

"Careful!" she shouted. "The rubble could shift!"

Three of the nearest Terrans turned briefly to stare in her direction, but the rest of them ignored her, and some of them seemed to be fixated on the work of the guardians, the metal golem's machine hands scrambling at the broken walls of the building. Servos whirred, chunks of burned and blackened permacrete tumbled, and the Commander oversaw it all, watching the guardians clear the way.

Something moved.

Suddenly the other Terrans rushed in, some of them grabbing at a form just out of sight. A body was pulled out of the newly formed pit and placed on a hovering stretcher. The hands were badly burned, but the face was still recognizable, as if this person had covered their eyes when the firestorm began. Unconscious eyes flicked open, and that was when the injured Terran uttered a low, rasping noise that rose in crescendo until it was a wavering scream.

The sound of it caused Mitsuki to cover her mouth. Guillermo reached back and grasped at her other arm which hung loose at her side.

Soon several other survivors were being carried out of the pit, many of them women and children, and many were covered in grime and some had burns and other horrific injuries. The victims stared at the soldiers and automata with bewildered looks, many of them with expressions of shock and fear. They had been through hell, and some of them struggled against the soldiers only to be sedated by medical personnel and hauled away on the hovering stretchers.

"Take these survivors to the med-bay," the Commander ordered. "See that they get the best care. We must wait to question them until after they are healed."

"But commander," said one young soldier, his skull-form face shield down to cloak his expression. "We must have answers. We must find the perpetrators of this crime before they strike again. Perhaps the victims can provide answers."

"All in good time, ensign," she said, her face a mask. "The Shibboleth who did this will face justice for what they have done. Rest assured. I will not stop until every last one of them lies screaming beneath my boot heel."

With a silent signal, the rest of the main force went to work, aiding the guardians to clear away more rubble in search of more survivors. Ivory and Guillermo turned to find Mitsuki sitting on the remains of a wall, her face buried reservedly in her hands.

"What about our family?" she asked, her voice nearly a whisper.

Ivory stood silent for a moment, her eyes scanning the ground.

"It appears," she said, biting her lip before she continued. "Your relatives were not among the survivors we rescued. If they had been, I would have pointed them out to you. I am sorry."

Mitsuki stared at the Commander, tears welling up in her eyes. She grit her teeth. She had lived a life of tragedy, living alone on Ontocca for most of her life. She never met her parents, and now it seemed that she never would.

Guillermo, accustomed to grief, sat next to Mitsuki on the desecrated wall.

"Whatever you need I'll help you," Mitsuki murmured. "Whatever it takes."

"Let's get back to the ship," Guillermo said. "There's really nothing more we can do here. I always assumed the Shibboleth were peaceful, but if I...if we...can do something about it by working with you, then we will do what we can."

Mitsuki looked at him then, her eyes welling with tears.

"We have to," she said. "The children...there were so many children."

She became silent then, almost reverting back to the way he had found her on Ontocca, back when she lived alone in the jungle. She stared at him, her mouth opening to form a word but then closing again. She only took his hand for a brief moment before letting it go and turning to walk away.

Mitsuki's familiar smirk had been drowned by the grimy black residue of blinding white anger, and this anger bled over to feed Guillermo's rage. He watched Mitsuki walk back to the landing ramp of the shuttle, watched her board and disappear from view before turning to face the Commander again.

"Keep looking for our family," he said, his face a chiseled block of stone as he watched the troopers sift through the rubble. "I think I could find a way to bear losing my family after all this time, after all I've been through, but she can't. She's too fragile. She might be great in a fight, but deep down she's like a child in a lot of ways. She needed this. She needed to find her grandparents."

Commander Ivory placed her hands on Guillermo's broad shoulders.

"I assure you," she said calmly, her eyes studying his. "I will do everything in my power to find them, and if I don't I will do everything in my power to bring these monsters to justice."

Guillermo nodded, pulled away from the Commander, and walked slowly to another shuttle that was landing nearby. She looked on, pausing a moment to watch him before a new problem arose for which she had to devise orders.

13

Guillermo and Mitsuki solemnly returned to their new quarters, two spartan rooms twelve floors above the engineering section, aft of the main shuttle hangar. The rooms consisted of a small bed, a wash station, a minuscule latrine and two portholes facing the dark blanket of space. Guillermo stepped inside his room for one moment, sniffed the stale air, then popped back out into the hall to rap repeatedly on Mitsuki's door.

The portal slid aside and Mitsuki stood staring at him with heavy-lidded eyes.

"Can we not get some rest before you need something?" she asked.

"No," he said, his hands waving emphatically. "I just wanted to decompress about that planet...what happened down there. I have to talk about it."

"What do you mean?" she asked as he shuffled inside her room to plop onto her bed. "The part about meeting our families who may or may not be dead or the part about all the innocent dead?"

"I mean that these Shibboleth were not who we were originally led to believe they were," he said. "Makes me wonder what other lies we were told. And like I said...If we are connected to them..."

She folded her arms.

"What do you mean?"

"Well," he replied. "Back on Ontocca old Zuraal told me that I was a child of the Shibboleth, that we both were. If we are to believe our new friends, then we have to believe that we were born into a terrorist organization. But I can't tell them that. Who knows what they'll do?"

"I...I just can't believe that our entire idea of the Shibboleth...of who we are is a lie."

"But the mining colony!" he said. "You saw the attackers on the holo-projector. We were under attack for some time... and our families...they still haven't reported back to us about it."

She reached inside her jacket which hung across a chair and pulled out a small rectangular object, a bound sheaf of paper, something he hadn't seen in ages, wrapped in a wrinkled cover of fire-blackened animal hide. As she removed it, little crumbs of brittle leather sloughed off of it and sprinkled the floor beneath her jacket. She held it up to the light, examining it a bit before handing it to him. He took it from her gently in his mechanical hand, turning it over and over.

"There's no markings on this...book," he said. "What is it? I don't dare open it. Might fall to pieces."

"Pretty badly burned," she replied, her voice soft. "Looks like some kind of journal or something. I found it in the wreckage but I didn't bother to look inside. Thought I'd get back to the room before I looked at it."

She sat on the bed next to him and he lay the little book between them. Little flakes of blackened leather fell from it when he moved it. Guillermo looked near the bed and found a little sliver of metal on a nearby table, a stylus for a holographic display he supposed. He slipped it between the damaged pages, the crinkle of crisped paper the only sound in the cold room.

"I haven't seen one of these in so long. The Bugs had one in the museum at the capital. Apparently people used to write things down and print them on these. Holographic documents are much less fragile. Information can be stored on the smallest thing, even duraglass filament plates, smaller than a human cell...or even on DNA."

"Sure," she said. "But people like to feel a book in their hand...the pages."

He frowned at her, shaking his head.

"Yeah. So let's look inside it and see what we can..."

He paused, both of them staring at the words on the page, only legible in the center as the edges were so badly burned.

"This is a religious text," Guillermo said. "Not really sure what kind. They kind of all look the same, or so I'm told."

She picked up the little book and examined it carefully, reading a few lines from the center of the page.

"I have spread out my hands all day long to a rebellious people...who walk in the way which is not good, following their own thoughts..."

She paused and they stared at each other for a moment, eyes locked.

"Not a clue," said Guillermo finally, and this wrenched a small laugh from Mitsuki.

Guillermo actually felt a tinge of joy at the little laugh, even though it seemed strained and somehow forced.

She turned a few crinkled pages and read again.

"Truly, truly, I say to you, we speak of what we know and testify of what we have seen, and you do not accept our testimony. If I told you earthly things and you do not believe, how will you believe if I tell you heavenly things?"

"Okay," Guillermo interrupted, placing a hand gently on

her arm. "So what do we know and testify to? It's talking about heaven and earth...one thing that is mythology and the other that is a burned out, used up globe our people left centuries ago. This thing sounds like any other religious text I've heard. Is there a mention of any religious figure or god in there?"

She turned a few more cracked pages, and one of them fell out in her hand. She flipped it over and held it close to her eyes before backing it away and reading the words found there.

"At that time Jesus said, 'I praise you, Father, Lord of heaven and earth, because you have hidden these things from the wise and learned, and revealed them to little children.'."

Guillermo snapped his metallic fingers, the sound making a strange thunking clang.

"Jesus!" he shouted. "Pretty sure I've heard that name before, but not really sure."

"Jesus," Mitsuki repeated. "That name is...I should know that name. I've heard it before, too."

They sat in silence a little while longer, the only sound the soft, far-away rumble of the ship's engines.

"Weren't religious texts banned during the reign of the Phaedran Empire?" Guillermo asked. "How did this thing survive that?"

Mitsuki only shrugged, gripping the small book gently in her hands.

"And what was it doing at a Terran mining colony on the other side of the ion cloud?" she asked.

"No idea," he said. "But I think our new acquaintances might be able to shed some light on that. You think? Or should we show them?"

"I don't know," Mitsuki said, shaking her head. "I'm confused by the way the survivors reacted to the soldiers."

"They were in shock," Guillermo said, his metallic hand on

the small book. "If you just had your town burned to a crisp you'd be pretty frightened, too...even of your rescuers."

Suddenly there was a sound, a whirring of energy crackling in the room. A small pinpoint of light appeared and then unfolded into a reflective sphere, but Guillermo knew that the reflection was actually the other side of a small wormhole. Seconds later Chief Engineer Adanez stood before them, her chest heaving with exhaustion, her eyes wide as if she had just seen a ghost.

"Don't be alarmed," she said, holding one gloved hand out. "I was able to use the transport emitter internally... something I've been working on...but we don't have much time. I've been sent by the Shibboleth to get you out of here."

Guillermo balled up his fist.

14

Dervish, sinking to her knees, stared at the Queen who had steepled her claw-like fingers and was staring at her across Dr. Spurling's desk.

Her presence was impossible. Illogical.

How could she have found her way through the ion cloud without damaging her ship, without killing all of her crew? Dervish scanned the room for an exit, formulated a foolhardy plan, and then spoke to her former queen with a pheromonal cue and body language that exuded disgust.

<You betrayed all that we are as a race,> Dervish signed. <Your armies have conquered probably the entirety of the Five Rims by now, and for what?>

<Indeed> replied the Queen, her damaged mandible, only a stub, wiggling like a small worm on her face. <I sought you out, my palace guard. I sought you so that I could mend our hive together. Bring you back into the fold. Luckily my colleagues, these Terran Phaedrans, stumbled upon Guillermo and Mitsuki floating in space and contacted me immediately. Our alliance is indeed strong.>

<Guillermo was right! You have allied yourself with the Phaedran Empire!> Dervish clicked. <They who subjugated us

for centuries! You are a traitor to our kind...to all the races of the Five Rims!>

Dr. Spurling, brushing a small bit of lint from his sleeve, stepped over to stand beside the desk. He placed one hand on the shiny onyx surface and spread his fingers out like a star.

"Your communication method is not conducive to a fair conversation," he said. "Please use Terran from here-on-out."

Both of the bugs turned their heads slowly to stare at the Doctor. He only folded his arms.

"As you suggest," chittered the Queen. "We will accommodate our alliance as agreed."

Dervish rose to her feet, her hand covering the oozing wound in her side. The nanites didn't seem to be working as they had in the past.

"Oh yes," said the Doctor. "I neutralized the nanites in your system once you exited the protective barrier of the surgery room. I thought your health might be a good bargaining chip for this very meeting...which I predicted would be inevitable."

"How long have you been working with the Pheadrans?" Dervish asked. "How long!"

"Since the day their spy, Ivy Salbura, approached me in the palace, removed her disguise, and proceeded to tell me the truth about her kind. I realized that we must bury any old hatreds, work together to find common ground. They control all space beyond the ionic cloud and we now control the other side. It is a mutual arrangement."

"You are lying," hissed Dervish. "There is another reason."

The Queen and the Doctor looked at each other briefly, as if the Queen were looking for some kind of non-verbal cue from him.

"This bodyguard was bred for her intelligence and strong reasoning skills," the Queen explained as if looking at a germ under a microscope. "She had to learn to know her place in the caste."

Dervish, seeing her chance, leaped forward, shooting across the desk. She immediately slammed into a crackling and painful energy shield that shimmered like an orange wall of light. As she fell to the floor, the Queen stood from her seat and stared down at Dervish.

"You have much to learn about this alliance, palace guard. In time you will see that it is the best way to ensure our survival. We must co-exist with the Phaedran's leader or face extinction."

Dervish turned to look at the Doctor who was moving toward her, producing a hyper-syringe from his jacket pocket.

"Her majesty understands the gravity of not complying with the wishes of the Most High Computat. His Conduit will be arriving shortly, and we will use the information locked in the mind of the fugitive Terrans to wipe out the Shibboleth once and for all and to finally ascend from this mortal plane."

"I will fight you," said Dervish, struggling to stand.

"It is inevitable that you must," he said. "But understand that you will indeed fail."

Dervish turned away, placing one claw-like hand on the desk. She could feel the energy shield crackling near her, but the Doctor was moving beyond it, nearing her with blind arrogance. With rising fortitude she kicked the Doctor across the room where he slammed against the wall and lay motionless. The Queen immediately produced a length of metal that rapidly extended and produced an electrified blade on the end. She used it to strike at Dervish who barely managed to duck beneath as it crackled overhead.

Dervish fell back, attempting to draw the Queen over the desk and out of range of the energy shield. The Queen took the bait, leaping over the table and jabbing the blade at

Dervish who dropped to the floor and sprung across to grab at the Queen's knees. This tactic luckily didn't backfire, and she toppled the Queen to the floor.

Rather than strike back, Dervish leaped to the ceiling, ripped the slatted cover from an air vent, and squeezed herself inside.

15

Guillermo pushed Mitsuki behind him in a protective manner and her face became a picture of annoyed anger.

"Shibboleth!" he shouted. "But you wiped out an entire colony —"

"—It was not us," Adanez protested calmly, holding up one trembling hand. "I risked everything to have this meeting, knowing that the events that unfolded at the colony would soon compromise my cover. They have filled your mind with lies. The Shibboleth they captured will soon succumb to the mind probes of Dr. Spurling. Right now I don't know how much time we have before the guardians figure out I'm gone. They swim in these metal walls like predatory fish in water."

Guillermo took a step back as Mitsuki shoved his arm away and stepped within inches of Adanez.

"So what is the truth?" she said, her nostrils flaring. "We saw what your people did on that planet...what they did to my family!"

Clover Adanez blinked her brown eyes and then her mouth opened wide as she took in a breath, a breath that began to hitch as she fought back a wave of emotion.

"My sister was down there," she said, large tears rolling down her face. "That was a secret Shibboleth colony...and my sister...her husband...everyone is gone. You have to know the truth. You have to realize what you mean to us... that your family has been long dead...killed by the Phaedran death squads."

Adanez collapsed into a nearby chair and Mitsuki reached for her but she put up one hand in defense. Mitsuki took the engineer's hand and helped her to her feet.

"I don't know who to believe," Mitsuki said, her face a blank mask. "My grandparents..."

Guillermo cleared his throat and then placed his hands on his head.

"Can someone please tell me the truth around here?"

Mitsuki gave Guillermo a sardonic glance.

"What proof do you have, Adanez?" she asked.

Adanez stood to her feet, and with shaking hands produced a small holographic emitter.

"I don't have much time, but what I'm about to show you will explain everything. You'll see what we are up against, and when and if the Shibboleth world ship can dislodge itself from other-space we can get away with them. You two are part of a greater defense against them. You'll see."

She flipped a control stud on the emitter.

"This was recorded yesterday," she said.

Before Guillermo could offer a retort, an image of Commander Ivory appeared before them. She sat at a console where she called up another holographic image of a floating head. The eyes were two large mechanical lenses that protruded from wrinkled and withered flesh, the mouth a vapid line. Various metal tines protruded from his hairless scalp like a halo of black thorns. His cracked lips shrank and deformed into a dry and hateful frown.

"Conduit Plath," said the Commander, her voice steady

and mechanical. "You summoned me."

"The Most High Computat is pleased that you have found two of the children lost to us," said the metallic modulated voice of the elder, his harsh eyes like two binocular lenses focusing in and out with a whirring noise. "Has Doctor Spurling neutralized the nanites in the male's system?"

"The code is very advanced, Conduit," said Ivory, her eyes downcast. "It has overridden every attempt to countermand it. We need a direct line to the Most High Computat for more clarity."

"That will never be allowed," said the Conduit, his fissured lips moving over rotting teeth. "But this is an opportunity not to be wasted. If you wish to ascend to our office you must learn to make the most of opportunities like this."

"Yes, Conduit Plath. I will not fail you. I have been sewing seeds of trust with them, fabricating a hunt for their family on the Shibboleth colony we recently destroyed."

A wheezing modulated laugh sounded then, and Guillermo felt his stomach churn.

"Of course you will not fail me," said the Conduit. "Our survival is at stake, but more immediately the survival of you and your crew. We have found another Shibboleth colony not far from your position. Perhaps you should stage an exercise and then devise a strategy to win the hearts of the newcomers...let them avenge the deaths of their imaginary family."

"I have already had the medical crew dress a body to pose as the male's mother."

Mitsuki gasped. Guillermo cleared his throat and then dented the wall with his metal fist before stalking away.

"Excellent," Plath grinned. "Any success with the bug guard?"

"Dr. Spurling is making progress with her. And the Queen is cooperating, helping us without realization of the truth.

She believes we are helping her take back her ancestral territory."

"This strategy pleases the Most High Computat," interrupted the Conduit boorishly. "Our deception is nearly complete. If the bug guard will not comply with our experimentation, if it is a waste of resources, then she must be terminated. If the Terrans you rescued will not comply with our plans for them, then they must be placed in stasis until we can bring them to Phaedra Prime. Find out what you can. That is all."

The image winked out as Adanez closed down the holo emitter and put it away. Before she, Guillermo or Mitsuki could speak the alarms began to wail.

16

"There is a hangar bay a few decks down from here," shouted Adanez over the blare of the alarm klaxon. "Our worldship should emerge from other-space soon."

"What are these alarms?" barked Guillermo, pacing the floor. "I want to kill all of these v'oshtu!Are they on to you?"

"That is highly unlikely. Perhaps the bug they brought aboard when they rescued you has escaped. We can't take chances, though."

"The bug?" exclaimed Guillermo as Mitsuki moved quickly to the wall expecting it to divide to create a door. It didn't.

"Yes," Adanez said. "I have disabled the slave circuit that controls her."

Guillermo's mind reeled with thoughts of Dervish. She had to be the bug Adanez mentioned. If she had escaped, then was she still hell-bent on killing him, on finishing the job for which she had been tasked?

Clover ignored them both, focusing on the problem. She approached the door and then waved her hand over the control panel, but it only flashed red. They were locked in, and with a nod to each other they all knew this truth.

"Can we use that wormhole transporter you used to get in here to escape to the hangar bay?" Mitsuki asked.

"It was a one way trip," Adanez explained. "Not enough power in the gauntlet to move us all, and that's too far anyway. By the time they figure out what has happened to the ship's internal systems, and who is to blame, we will hopefully be out of here. But my job is done here. Your lives mean much more to us than to the Phaedrans. All they want you for is ascendance, while we need you to help us get to Eden."

Guillermo stared at her for a second, not registering what she just said, and then shook his head.

"So what do we do?" Guillermo growled, his hands forming fists. "We don't have weapons, we don't have a way out of this room, and Dervish is apparently running around the ship being chased by the Phaedrans…or looking to kill us."

Adanez said nothing, only raising her arm to then waving her hand over a holographic display that flickered and then solidified above her wrist. They felt a jolt as something very large exploded within the ship far from their position.

And then they were in total darkness for a moment until faint emergency lighting winked on.

"Ok, that worked," Adanez said, her mouth turning down, her eyes darting left and right. "Now, let's get to work on that door."

Adanez approached the wall where she used her holographic wrist computer to access a few pre-written subroutines.

"We've been planning this ever since we learned of the massacre on the Bug home world. Now we just have to get you to the world ship. I'm pretty sure the 'we' is an 'I' by now, however. The two others in our little sleeper cell will surely not be joining us, but that's what they signed up for."

There was an electronic warble and suddenly the wall split open to reveal a dim corridor beyond. In the faint emergency lights they saw the silhouette of five automata and one very large Terran, his skin tattooed with skeletal designs, his thick grey hair in a topknot.

Before she could operate the door again, Adanez was hoisted from the floor by one of the automata and then carried into the room by her neck. Security Chief Absalom Liberty lurched into the room behind her, his automata guardians following, and with a flick of his wrist the skeletal tattoos began to glow a bright green as they emerged from his skin to form a crackling energy shield.

"Traitors," he grunted, his steely eyes reflecting the green glow of the energy shield. "Take her to the interrogation room immediately and bring the two of them as well. I'm sure we will be interested to find out what this traitor knows."

Guillermo shifted on his feet, glancing at Mitsuki who was already moving toward Adanez.

"I don't know what this is about," Guillermo said, his voice even. "Drop Adanez and we can talk this out. She's given us some information about your commander that bodes a second look."

The security chief smiled, the green skull face of the energy shield floating over his features mimicking the gesture.

"Your apparent amnesia has clouded your mind, brother," boomed Liberty. "If you knew of what you were capable, you would challenge me like the soldier you were born to be...or are you a traitor as well?"

The automata reacted then, not to the situation in the room, but to a thumping that echoed overhead. A lean form dropped from an air vent in the ceiling. At first it dropped to a crouch, then stood erect. In the dim light Guillermo watched in amazement as Dervish, her mottled red arms and legs now augmented with embedded metallic rods, tore into two nearby automata like a buzz saw.

The guardian holding Adanez tried to fight Dervish with one unarmed hand, but was no match for her strength as she grabbed its wrist, spun, and severed the limb from its metal body. Liberty wheeled on her, charging forward to shoulder-ram her to the deck plating and then roar like an animal. Guillermo darted forward then, leaping onto the back of the security chief as two more automata charged at Mitsuki in an attempt to subdue her. Mitsuki shifted down and to the side, but they were too fast for her, grabbing her by the wrists and pulling her toward the door.

Guillermo felt like he had leapt onto a wild animal whose back was covered with a blazing electrical fire. The security chief screamed and reached back to grab handfuls of Guillermo's shirt, pulling with such force that the shirt ripped from his body. Guillermo pounded with his metallic fist at the side of Liberty's head but only connected with the energy shield as it crackled and sparked green energy.

A strangely shrill laugh erupted from Liberty's barrel chest.

"You have not been trained in the ways of the techno-warrior!" Liberty growled. "And it will be your undoing."

Guillermo put his metallic arm around the security chief's throat and used every ounce of strength to constrict his air flow, but saw only sparks as the green energy shield surrounding him deflected his attempt. The security chief grabbed at the arm and pulled, slapping Guillermo to the deck like a wet rag.

"That all you got?" wheezed Guillermo, and with a sudden kick struck at Absalom's shin. Rising, he uppercutted the security chief but only glanced off of the energy shield, green sparks lighting the dim room.

A wave of energy ballooned out from Guillermo's left, a blinding blue flash that struck the security chief and caused him to wail more out of anger than pain. Guillermo blinked and then turned to see Adanez with a small pulse weapon aimed at Absalom. She was readying another blast, but Guillermo took the hint, charging at Absalom with metal fist cocking back. He pounded Absalom's thick chest, the security chief offering only a devilish grin.

A serrated blade suddenly erupted from the security chief's right shoulder and the energy shield flickered as Absalom looked at the blade in surprise. Dervish stood on the other side of him, a length of metal spear in her hands, and she was twisting the blade.

Dervish charged through the strewn pieces of automata on the floor, driving the security chief to the wall to pin him there. He grunted, squirming, reaching for the blade with one hand and turning his head to scream an unintelligible curse.

"This will not stop us," he howled. "If you escape you will be captured. It is the will of the High Computat. All see what I see. Your escape is already being headed off."

At his last word, more chrome plated guardians emerged from the walls. Adanez paused, briefly fiddling with her pulse pistol, her mouth moving in a silent count, and then with squinting eyes threw it at her enemies.

"Let's get out of here!" she shouted. "The hangar is not far. Follow me!"

They all darted out the door, closely followed by the automata, but the guardians were thrown against the opposite wall of the corridor by the blinding flash of the exploding pulse pistol. As the four of them quickly raced down the hall the hulking figure of Absalom emerged from the smoking doorway of Guillermo's quarters, wrenched the spear from his shoulder, and then uttered a primal shout which reverberated from the walls of the corridor.

17

"What the chert was he?" screamed Guillermo as they raced down the corridor toward the hangar bay.

His question was punctuated by the feral scream of Absalom far behind them.

"Shock troop," Adanez said, her breathing heavy and strained. "Techno-warrior fully augmented by the High Computat."

They arrived at a recessed section of the wall where Adanez now worked feverishly on her holographic display to open the locked portal to the hangar bay. The wrist display shifted from green to red as her face became a wan mask.

"They've locked me out," she said. "This may take longer than I thought. You guys up to fending off the —"

Three automata emerged from a nearby wall before she could finish her sentence, and the three other Terrans each grabbed a sparring partner. Guillermo struck at one of them with his metal fist and crushed its head against the wall as Dervish grabbed hers by the waist. With a twist of her body she was able to suplex the guardian into a nearby wall. Mitsuki struggled with hers, kicking and wrestling, before falling backward and using her feet to launch it down the hallway. As her automata rose to charge again, Absalom Liberty appeared, a green skeletal ghost outlining his form as he stalked toward them followed by several more guardians.

"Do not resist us!" he shouted. "Give up and maybe we will let the engineer and the bug live. You cannot escape this ship."

"Adanez, you think you could get that door open now?" Guillermo whispered out the side of his mouth, then loudly down the hall: "We loved the food and all... and the hospitality, but I think we've worn out our welcome here."

Guillermo spun to face Adanez.

"Any day now!"

A long cable shot down the hallway. Like a metallic tentacle it wrapped around her leg, dragging her clawing and struggling toward Absalom who reeled in the cable like a fishing line.

"This one will suffer!" screamed the green-haloed security chief.

A rage began to bubble in Guillermo's brain and he balled up his fists and grit his teeth. Mitsuki watched as amber lines of light began to emerge from his flesh, from his spine and rib cage. Bright orange flames erupted from his eyes. He charged down the hallway, screaming, closing the distance between Dervish and Absalom. As the automata attempted to encircle the security chief, Guillermo leaped into the air and with one swipe of the side of his metal hand severed the cable dragging Dervish to her doom.

"At last!" screamed Absalom. "You have embraced your inner truth!"

Guillermo roared, grabbed the severed cable with one hand, and with one swift motion he pulled Absalom to the deck. Automata came at him then, and when he but touched them with his metal arm they shattered like so much glass.

"Guillermo!" Mitsuki screamed. "Guillermo!"

But Guillermo was a wild animal, shredding automata as they raced down the hall and appeared out of the walls, ceiling and floor. It was a blinding flash of destruction that defied physics, as if his body were surrounded by its own strange, swirling system of gravity. Parts of the automata floated near him as if the artificial gravity could not register the weight of objects, and the security chief was trying to get to his feet but was unable to dodge the mass of mechanical body parts raining down on him like steel hail. The walls around Guillermo buckled outward with the strain and Guillermo's feral roar was the only thing that could be heard over the din.

Adanez shouted as the door to the hangar bay suddenly opened, and Dervish struggled to her feet.

"Guillermo!" Mitsuki screamed again, but he was in a frenzy.

She rushed forward, the whirling debris of the automata cutting her flesh, and she closed her eyes and reached for Guillermo just as one of the severed arms of the automata sliced deeply into her forearm. Guillermo was in a blind rage, the debris swirling about him, his back to her, his fists out at his sides as his shoulders heaved with his rapid breathing.

"Guillermo!" she screamed again, and this time he turned, his orange eyes ablaze. Just beyond him, Absalom struggled to stand.

"This is your true nature!" growled Absalom over the roar of the raining metal. "You will show us all how to ascend as you were born to do!"

Mitsuki did not shrink back, but drove forward, the metal slicing her skin again. She was then hit on the head by a chunk of metal, nearly blacking out, but then Guillermo had her in his arms. He carried her out, bursting through a thick durasteel wall to the hangar bay as they raced toward a transport ship sitting empty on the deck.

18

"Can you fly this thing, bug?" Adanez shouted as she dashed toward the lowered entrance ramp on the shuttle. "I'll get the engines fired up if you can manage the stick!"

Dervish managed a limping jog and only nodded the affirmative as Guillermo set Mitsuki carefully to the deck. She nodded at him in quiet communication as he turned to the hangar bay door where several automata were marching through. Mitsuki rushed to the ship, not looking back, the wounds from the hallway outside making her clothing stiff with her own blood. As she ascended the landing ramp she found a small cache of plasma rifles just within. She grabbed one and stood in the door to help Guillermo froze. The automata had charged him, surrounded him, but they were quickly batted away by Guillermo's fierce and raging fists.

"Help the engineer with the engines," Guillermo said, his teeth set on edge. "I'll take care of these goons."

Just as she turned away, a feral roar was heard at the doorway to the hangar. She turned to see the security chief barreling through into the hangar. His own energy shield turned the decking around him green as he sprinted forward, arms out to his sides, fingers spread like the claws of an

Ontoccan cave bear.

Guillermo destroyed one guardian with a swipe of his hand then set his feet on the deck, knees bent, hands balling into fists. The energy crackled around him and his eyes glowed a bright amber. She felt helpless to stop him, to get him to flee with them.

"Guillermo!" she shouted. "Get on the ship!"

Guillermo seemed to ignore her as the security chief closed the distance.

"I have him," Guillermo snarled. "I can kill him....end this!"

She limped toward him, plasma rifle raised. The shuttle's engines powered up and the glow of the thrusters sent bits of dust flying in all directions. She reached for his arm but pulled back in pain when the amber shield sparked and burned her fingers.

"Guillermo!" she shouted. "Please!"

The security chief dropped low at the end of his run and slid across the floor, attempting to take Guillermo out at the knees. Guillermo side-stepped, gave Absalom a right cross with a prepared metal fist, but Absalom's body careened into Mitsuki, sending both of them rolling in a mass to the deck. Guillermo turned, his eyes on fire, and grabbed the security chief, dragging him away. Mitsuki's unconscious form snapped him back to sanity.

With one motion, his personal shield subsiding, he scooped up Mitsuki and ran to the waiting landing ramp to board the shuttle. The ramp raised as he ran on into the ship, and once inside he immediately lay Mitsuki on a circular couch. The pinging of metal arms could be heard banging on the hull of the shuttle and Guillermo absently wondered why they didn't just phase through like they could on the main ship.

"In here!" came Dervish's raspy voice.

Guillermo raced to the cockpit.

"I need some help getting this thing off the ground," she said. "If what I read here is correct, we are going to have company as soon as we launch. They have already scrambled several fighters in anticipation of our escape."

"They aren't all for us," wheezed Adanez as she stumbled into the cockpit with them, out of breath. "They have picked up our world ship sliding through hyperspace to our location...probably leaking a trail of plasma as well..."

The engineer reached past Guillermo and Dervish to activate a few control studs. She pressed an activation switch to erect the shielding just as an explosion rocked their shuttle. The shuttle emitted a bright blue flash as its two plasma cannons punched a shuttle-sized hole through the door of the hangar bay ejecting all the automata into space with the remaining atmosphere.

"Why didn't you do that before?" Guillermo said, eyebrows raised.

She glanced at the outside scanners.

"Well, it didn't take care of Absalom," she murmured. "Heavens he's like a cockroach."

Guillermo could see the security chief's bio-signature as he held fast to a bulkhead door, but he was crawling along the wall to a nearby gunship.

"Those fighters are scrambled to take out our world-ship." Adanez said. "But let's pray to the God of the Universe that we can get the FTL engine running again for another jump before they do. The Phaedrans won't be able to shoot at us or lock a retrieval beam on us. I made sure to disable that before I jumped through that singularity and we have a limited amount of time before that gets restored. So punch it, Dervish."

Dervish waved her hand over some of the controls and the shuttle lurched forward as it rocketed out of the bay, immediately dropping a bit as it adjusted to the absence of artificial gravity. Their shuttle was surprisingly fast, but something rocked the ship, a powerful blast, and Guillermo noticed several angry blips on the scope.

Swooping in behind them, followed by a four-ship squadron of Phaedran fighters, came an imposing gunship, its bow molded to resemble a screaming skull, its wings bat-like and bristling with four plasma cannons each.

"We won't make that world ship if big and angry shoots us down," Guillermo said, slipping out of the cockpit to run aft.

"I'll see what I can do to make him think twice about it!"

As he bolted to the rear cannons, he passed a sleeping Mitsuki but did not stop. His mind was focused, but his fingers itched to use the guns.

19

Mitsuki woke to the sound of crackling power couplings, her eyelids fluttering at the sight of sparks coming from a nearby power relay. She shrunk back as they sprayed painfully across her arm. She brushed at it, suffering only minor burns as she tried to figure out her location.

"Oh yeah," she stammered, her memory coming back to her.

She rose, somewhat shakily as the inertial stabilizers seemed to be damaged, and she called out for someone, anyone, but no one answered. She looked the cockpit door and in the gloom could make out Dervish's clawed hand flicking control studs. Adanez was barking orders to her, correcting her understanding of the foreign flight controls. The bright bursts of light through the front view screen indicated that they were under attack. A heavy thud from aft of her position nearly caused her to stumble forward, and she could hear the familiar growls of Guillermo's Guajiin profanity echoing from down the opposite corridor.

"V'oshtus!" he screamed.

She looked around, noticing a sign marked "engineering" and followed that corridor down and around a curve until she emerged in a familiar space. The plasma fusion engines were expelling a foul smelling gas that she knew she had to get locked down.

A plasma bolt suddenly shot past her head and burned a black divot in the adjacent wall.

Someone had stowed away.

Two Phaedran males in full armor, their skull-visaged face-shields down, ran toward her with guns blazing as she rolled away and into a small recessed alcove near the door to the engineering room.

She looked around briefly, finding a heavy hydrostatic wrench. Uttering a bloody scream, she charged the two of them, managing to knock the rifle from the hands of the larger of the two assailants. It seemed that they were taken aback by this unassuming attacker, and the second Phaedran attempted to fire his rifle point blank at Mitsuki but she in turn grabbed the barrel and forced it toward the other Phaedran. It discharged and blasted a hole through the soldier's torso.

The dead Phaedran fell to deck with a thump as she brained the second one with her wrench and then continued to pound until he didn't move. She stood over them, shoulders rising and falling as she heard alarms sounding from the back wall of the engineering room. She ran to the source, dropping the damaged, bloody wrench to the floor.

The two Phaedrans had sabotaged the fuel inflow controls, most of the delicate fiber optic cables left dangling in disarray.

She blew a strand of hair out of her face with an updraft of air from her protruding bottom lip and went to work. She looked around for replacement circuits. She pulled out maintenance drawers completely from their alcoves and dumped them out on the floor as the ship shook with enemy fire. She kicked bits of repair parts across the decking, her voice a combination of mumbling and screaming until she found a few gel-pack circuit modules that might do the trick.

Alarms continued to sound, and she heard the pounding of the enemy plasma cannons as they sheared away sections of the outside hull. Sweat dripped from her nose as she finally figured out how to stop the sparking fuel supply conduits from gushing out hot plasma. The backup safety valves were near failure. She slammed the gel-packs in place, finding a laser welder hooked into a nearby wall port and then finally the out-gassing began to subside. She held her breath and moved her fingers over a control stud.

She let out a deep breath, then felt the hot sting of plasma fire on her right shoulder. She spun, her hand moving to the smoking wound, and saw the brained Phaedran rising to his feet on shaky legs, the plasma rifle quivering in his gloved hands.

She screamed something unintelligible, dropping low to charge forward. He fired one shot at her then, but missed, and she took the opportunity to close the gap, grabbing a nearby shipping container lid to use as a shield for the next plasma bolt. She cried out as a bit of molten slag dropped onto her thigh, burning through her clothing. In anger, she threw the lid like a discus and knocked the rifle from the Phaedran's hands, then ran at him and gave him a flying kick to the chest.

She crushed the Phaedran to the deck, and after a few seconds she rose slowly and staggered out of the engineering room, back into he common area. She could hear the frantic voices of her crew mates.

"There's the world-ship!" Adanez shouted from the cockpit. "Just get us in any of those hangar bays before the Phaedran mothership opens fire with the big cannons!"

"I thought you said you disabled them," came the strangely calm voice of Dervish.

"I did," she said. "But it won't be long now until they

figure out how to override my subroutines."

"They already have!" bellowed Guillermo from the aft corridor, his metallic arm smoking slightly, his face shining with sweat. "They hit the rear guns with something big. I hope they don't take out the engines with it."

Mitsuki only stared at him, her hand gripping her searing plasma wound. Guillermo gave her a sidelong glance as he passed her and ran to the cockpit.

"You can't sleep all day, Mitsuki," he said. "Go back to engineering and see if you can get things locked down."

He pointed to the engineering corridor impatiently and then flicked his hand for her to get busy.

"It's over there," he directed.

He only glanced at her one more time before he entered the cockpit and focused his attention on the world-ship ahead of them. Mitsuki offered a half-smile, her eyelids heavy, and turned slowly to traipse back to engineering as commanded.

20

The world ship appeared in space suddenly, its mushroom-shaped bulk squeezing out of what appeared to be a rounded, starless void. It was actually a wormhole that simply echoed what was on the other side, but instead of stars all that was visible was a sooty emptiness. It was as if the limping, drifting world-ship had emerged from a black velvet bag.

As soon as the ship appeared it was under attack, the Phaedran fighters swarming its long upside-down spires that stretched nearly the length of the central hub from beneath the rounded and overhanging top section. Ancient engines fired up, coughing out a white blast of energy that trailed bits of rusted and decayed hull plating and guide fins. A weak energy shield absorbed the plasma blasts from the fighters, but it sparkled and vibrated with a faint yellow light that dimmed with each successive strike from the superior Phaedran weapons.

Guillermo had only seen the grounded world-ship that had become Ontocca City. He couldn't believe this old hulk was still space-worthy. He placed a hand on Dervish's shoulder, wincing as they suffered yet another hit on their aft shields by the ambitious security chief.

"Can you get us through that?" he asked.

"I can try, Guillermo," she replied, her clawed hands flying over the controls.

Mitsuki appeared in the doorway to the cockpit.

"I was able to get things...locked down," she said, her mouth a twisted pout. "You can go back there and check if you want...I mean, if you don't trust me."

Guillermo gave her a quick glance and then focused his attention back on the world-ship ahead of them, and that was when a section of the starboard side of the massive ship erupted in a coughing cloud of debris, crushing inward. It began to list to the side, but no blast from any Phaedran craft had done the damage. It appeared instead to be self-inflicted.

"Ohhh it looks like that last jump ruptured one of the redundant power plants," Adanez said, her voice raised above the din. "We have to get on board and help the engineers. They're kind of green."

"I am doing what I can," Dervish said plainly, dodging another squadron of fighters. "But I will attempt not to fail us."

"Does this heap have any other guns aboard?" Guillermo asked, his metallic hand squeezing the bulkhead until it creaked.

"What happened to the aft gun?" asked Adanez.

"It was...damaged," Guillermo said. "...got shot off."

Adanez placed a grimy hand on Dervish's arm. Dervish seemed to ignore her, weaving and bobbing around the attacking swarm of Phaedran fighters.

"You get us in there, Bug," she said, turning to face Mitsuki. "Come with me."

Adanez pushed past Guillermo and Mitsuki followed. Guillermo fell out into the common area.

"What do you want me to do?" he shouted at Adanez.

She did not turn around, disappearing into the engineering

bay.

"Pray!" she shouted over her shoulder.

Guillermo stood silent for a second, then replied to the engineering hallway because she had already vanished down it.

"To who?!"

A few seconds later Adanez and Mitsuki rounded the corner into the engine room to find the dead Phaedrans and the cobbled together power couplings.

"What happened back here?" Adanez exclaimed.

Mitsuki didn't acknowledge the dead, only turned to face the engineer.

"What now?"

"Well, we need see if we can coax the shields on this heap to give us a little more time. You ready to do what I tell you?"

"Sure," Mitsuki said calmly. "Whatever you need."

Something thumped the outside of the ship and the lights flickered.

"You do all this?" Adanez said, pointing at the jury rigged conduits, to which Mitsuki only nodded.

"Not bad," Adanez offered. "Now get over there and calibrate that inflow while I adjust the output module."

In the cockpit, Guillermo plopped down next to Dervish, his hands flying over the controls to aid in propulsion and using the shield modulators to give them a little more protection as they weaved their way through the swarm of ships. Ahead of them the world-ship loomed, a trail of debris floating off in a line behind it. The shuttle suddenly lurched and then began to slow.

"Chert!" Dervish screamed. "Something's got us."

"I'll bet it's that ship behind us," Guillermo snapped, dialing up the aft scanner array.

His shoulders slumped.

"It's the mothership. She's back in business."

Just then a crackle of blue energy and sparks danced across the control panel in front of them, smoke filling the cockpit. Dervish and Guillermo raised their singed hands from the panel and watched as a heavy beam of plasma cut through the dark of space and caused the shields of the world-ship to glow and flicker. The yellow energy shield appeared to hover just over the hull of the world-ship before it faded to an amber static and then allowed the beam to pierce through, blasting a black crater in the pock-marked surface of the ancient durasteel.

Before any of them could react, another blast struck their shuttle and the two of them were thrown to the floor, a blanket of darkness suddenly falling over all of them. The emergency lights clicked on, humming to life as Mitsuki stumbled into the doorway of the cockpit.

"Come back to engineering," she said, out of breath. "All of you. Now."

21

Alarms sounded as they raced down the corridor to engineering. When they rounded the corner Adanez stood near the energy intake manifold, peering from behind welding goggles, each gloved hand holding a glowing cable. She drove the ends of them together and instantly a bright ball of fire erupted before her. She dove out of the way as the fire became a glowing sphere.

"Jump into that!" she shouted, wheezing out a breath. "If it works, we'll be safe in there."

"Safe in where?" Guillermo exclaimed. "And what do you mean 'if it works'?!"

"I think, if I got the calculations right, it leads to somewhere inside the world ship. But we have to go now."

They all stared at the glowing orb which fluctuated from green to blue and then stabilized into a wobbling silver orb. Guillermo could see a shape move, thinking at first it was his reflection but then it ran away from him as if he were viewing it through a fish-eye lens.

Mitsuki looked at Guillermo, then back at Adanez, then at Dervish, and ran toward the orb. Her hands touched it and it swallowed her up with a strange electric slurp. Something struck the ship again at that moment and they could hear the unmistakable sound of air escaping into a vacuum from somewhere toward the bow. It was the high squeal of a fissure crack somewhere.

The shields had most likely failed.

"Get in!" Adanez screamed again.

Dervish was next, followed by Guillermo who took a deep breath and then leaped in, his eyes wide. He felt a sensation something like drowning, but also like his lungs were full of squirming insects. Before he could gasp he found himself falling, right before striking an object that broke, something that cracked when his ribs struck it and then he was falling again...out of a tree and onto a patch of weedy grass.

He heard a groan as Adanez fell out of the tree behind him and landed on Guillermo's back.

"Sorry about that," she said. "At least we aren't in a bulkhead."

She stood up a little too fast because, staggering about a bit before getting her bearings. One second later she was running toward a nearby half-open door, the rusted metal panel stuck halfway into the wall. Guillermo stood just as Dervish and Mitsuki rushed over to help him up. Waving them off, he saw that he was in a large nursery where several trees grew in a large grove. It was a massive garden that stretched over an artificial hill and far above he could see the sporadic artificial sunlight, several of the immense panels broken and dark.

"Wait a minute," Guillermo muttered as he headed for the door. "Where is she going?"

The rest of them followed, Mitsuki limping a bit as she did her best to catch up, and soon they found Adanez standing at a closed bulkhead door frantically tapping away at a smudged and cracked control panel.

"We have to get to engineering immediately," she said,

typing her way through several flickering sub-routines. "The FTL drive is malfunctioning, but in a good way, and we need to get there to help out."

The door suddenly hissed open, the ancient servos groaning. Before them stood several Terrans, each of them eyes wide as they saw the four of them. The Terrans all reached for holstered weapons, one of them mumbling about "intruders", but then there was a shout from the back.

"Adanez!" came only a voice, and then a young man pushed his way through the crowd, his face smudged with grease, his blonde hair dirty and disheveled. "Thank God you made it! We need your help."

"Of course you do," she said matter-of-factly. "Take me to the problem. Don't tell me you broke my ship!"

The crowd parted and they were all soon running down another long corridor that slightly curved to the right and down. They emerged in a large chamber, several metallic and rusting pylons protruding from a spherical ceiling far above. The pylons all converged at the center of the cavernous room where a burned-out and sparking sphere rested on a greasy dais. Five Terrans in tattered, oily jumpsuits stood around it, each of them holding antiquated scanners in one hand and various tools in the other. They were trying to repair it... whatever it was.

"This is a mess," offered Adanez as she rummaged through a nearby tool box for a couple of fine-tuning tools. Just then an explosion rocked the ship, an echoing boom that caused bits of rusting durasteel to rain down on them, drifting down like burnt orange snow.

Guillermo and the others felt out of place as the technicians went to work, Adanez barking orders and the other techs following them. To Guillermo they looked very desperate.

Mitsuki looked at Guillermo, then at Adanez, and with trepidation spoke to what seemed a vacant room.

"We have to stop that gun from hitting us," she offered.

Adanez only turned for a second, shrugged, and then went back to barking orders as if ignoring the rest. Another blow from the super-laser boomed and the already dim lights illuminating the chamber flickered briefly.

"What can we do?" Guillermo said.

Adanez, crouching down near an open panel, two techs working on either side of her, turned briefly to show her reddening face.

"Mitsuki, you seem to be good in a pinch! What do you know about calibrating power couplings?"

Mitsuki didn't say a word, only moved to grab a multi-tool and stood ready.

"Just say the word," she replied.

"Great!" Adanez barked. "Holland! Take Guillermo and Dervish to the command deck. Then get yourself back down here. We can't have any guardians worm-holing inside this room. That would be the end."

"Yes ma'am," said Holland, turning to Guillermo. "Come with me."

Guillermo and the Dervish followed the young guard through the door and then into a lift which took them to another deck filled with frantic people, each of them moving their frenzied hands over heavily modified control panels. The crew stared at cobbled together holo-displays where various red lights flashed and flickered. A grizzled old man, his grey beard nearly to the middle of his chest, spun to face them as soon as the doors to the lift opened.

His face lit up with an unexpected smile.

"You have been found!" he shouted.

"Sir," said a woman at one of the screens. "We cannot take another strike from that weapon. And I detect wormholes forming on decks three and eighteen."

"Engineering," the old man growled. "Send the troops

down to eighteen immediately. We have to get that FTL up and running or we are doomed."

22

The deck plating rattled with the cavitation of another major blow from the powerful weapons striking the world ship. Frantic crew tried their best to keep vital systems online but the cavitation after every blow from the massive plasma cannon was becoming longer after each hit. Dervish had offered her assistance, and now stood beside one of the teenage bridge crew like a doting mother.

Guillermo was just about to help when he felt a firm hand on his arm.

"Come with us," said a skinny young woman with wild grey hair. Her dark eyes, crow's feet wrinkling her skin, seemed to bore right through him. "The Phaedrans are boarding us with their drones. Can you fight?"

"Depends on who you ask," said Guillermo. "Let's go."

He nodded at Dervish.

"That means you, too, girl."

Dervish didn't make a sound, only fell in behind Guillermo as they jogged through the bulkhead door and down the corridor to follow the surprisingly spry elderly woman and her five armed guards. They could have been her grandchildren, but they wore armor cobbled together from random plates of durasteel and carbon fiber weave.

"The automata have emerged in the armory," said the woman, her breathing remarkably even for someone of her age. "You'll have to get a gun from one of them and then do your best to —"

"I don't need a gun, lady," said Guillermo, his orange shielding flickering to life. "Just point me in the direction of the trouble."

A faint smile waxed across her face briefly, and they soon emerged into a large room where several rows of old-style rail rifles rested in racks on the walls. The cadre stopped, some of them gripping their guns so tightly one could hear the old metal creak. Suddenly one of the young soldiers fired at the ceiling, his mouth open in a scream, as an automata fell from above and pounced on him, driving him to the floor.

It's pounding metal fists drowned out the young man's screams.

Dervish fired a superheated carbon rod into the ceiling, the flame from the barrel illuminating a swarm of automata crawling there. Guillermo grabbed a rail gun from a nearby rack and powered it up, firing a bolt into the brainpan of the one attacking the young soldier.

"Get her to safety!" Guillermo shouted, looking back at the old woman, but she held a rail gun in her wrinkled hands and was firing bolt after bolt at the swarming automata, her face grim.

Dervish didn't waste time, handing off her weapon to a nearby Terran soldier before skittering up an nearby wall. With her newly augmented arms and legs giving her even greater strength and agility, she leaped from wall to ceiling to dislodge three of the drones, tearing one apart with ferocity. A few of them dropped down behind Guillermo, their chromed spears darting toward him, but their blades sparked and were driven back by his energy shield. He turned on them, unloading three bolts that skewered them and pinned them to a nearby wall. They worked loose, their liquid metal bodies sliding around the superheated carbon rods as they rushed forward again to engage the soldiers.

Another blast from the Phaedran mother ship vibrated the deck plating and the lights failed, leaving them all in a void of darkness save for the warm glow of Guillermo's energy shield and the fiery blue eyes of the automata. Guillermo worked quickly, dropping the rifle to the deck to charge in on the glowing blue eyes. He grasped at whatever he found there, tearing them from the deck and tossing them to the side.

Suddenly they could feel the deck vibrate again, but this time it was accompanied by a pressure change that told Guillermo the ship had suffered a critical atmospheric breach somewhere. He could hear the distinctive sound of bulkheads closing, their power independent of the ship for safety concerns such as this, and he knew that they would soon be trapped in this room with the automata.

"Get out of this room now!" he shouted.

As he fought his way to the door, he could see it begin to inch shut, its ancient and rusting cogs desperately trying to close the breach. He barreled toward the door and placed himself in the way, the heavy door beginning to close in on him. He gripped the edge of the door, his armored back sparking and flashing energy as he strained at the metal portal. Several of the soldiers helped the elderly woman squeeze past him and into the hallway beyond, but he could hear the ancient gears grinding as he roared to the remaining soldiers to get out.

And then another blast from the Phaedran ship tore a hole in the hull on the far side of the armory.

23

Decompression was abrupt, the automata struggling to hang on to the floor, their feet sprouting sharp appendages that pierced the rusting metal of the deck plates. Some of them did not react in time and were pulled from the room and through the gaping hole on the other side of the room along with three of the unfortunate remaining Terran soldiers. Rifles, ancient flak armor and heavy crates began to lift from the floor and strike against the few standing automata left in the room, a few of them being driven back, uprooting them from the floor.

Dervish grabbed his arm.

Atmosphere rushed past Guillermo, one hand bracing on the door frame and the other pulling Dervish to him, her tree-toed feet dangling toward the yawning void on the other side of the room. He caught her arm, dragging her through, her strong legs clinging to the wall and then bracing against the corridor on the other side of the bulkhead. Guillermo's face contorted as he strained to pull himself through and allow the old door to close behind him.

He heard the ancient gears grind as he held fast on the other side of the door frame, but it inched slowly on, stopping with a whine and a rusty metal pop. Only a small gap remained where the atmosphere continued to whistle through.

"We have to seal it!" Guillermo screamed, turning to face Dervish, his eyes turning red.

Dervish looked back down to the other end of the hallway and spied the sealed bulkhead not far away. Without a visible acknowledgement she began to inch her way toward it.

"It will be shut tight!" screamed Guillermo. "Emergency lock is engaged!"

She ignored him, and as Guillermo tried to push himself forward away from the broken door, two sets of metallic hands reached through the small gap in the door. He could hear the servos grind as the automata tried to force their way in. He glanced back at Dervish who had already pulled the control panel from the wall and was busy rerouting wires with one hand as she held on with both feet and her other arm.

But she was slipping, and the air was vanishing, being replaced by the vacuum of space. His lungs felt like they were on fire and the temperature in the hallway dropped dramatically. With his metal fist he pounded at the robotic fingers. His ears popped as the pressure fell, and he felt his body begin to seize as the temperature plummeted.

And then it didn't matter.

He felt a sudden surge of energy course through him, but his arms and legs lost all feeling and his body fell limp. He floated backward, the gravity generators failing in the hallway, and he closed his eyes just as he was pulled along by a clawed hand. He tried to look behind him to see who was moving him, but he couldn't turn his head. When he opened his eyes he saw only white spots on a black background, like he was seeing hundreds of gigantic stars all clustered together.

Just as he was being pulled through the now open second bulkhead door, a vibrating hum rocked the entire deck, and then they were in the low silence of FTL travel.

24

Far away, deep within the realm beyond the ion cloud a solitary wasteland of a world spun around a binary star. On a forgotten plain surrounded by distant plateaus a pock-marked road traced a jagged line across the sand. Little wispy imps of wind-swept sand danced across it, nothing more than a well trafficked path across a oven-baked desert. It was a path where on many nights blood was spilled and screams cracked the oppressively thin air. A lone bounty hunter slouched along, heavy boots kicking up more dust, the thick, frayed, and rough-hewn cloth wrapping a solitary slender form. The survival suit designed for deep desert use clung mummy-like with long dirty strips flapping in the unforgiving air. The inexorable wind blasted everything with a poisonous smog unlike anything ancient Earth could produce.

The air here was breathable, but slightly toxic, enough to require added oxygen mined from prehistoric chunks of ice far below the surface. A high price was required for such luxury, but most, like the bounty hunter, used a device worn on the shoulders which used small domes filled with fungus coupled with filters to strain out the spores.

The bounty hunter wore a large brim black hat over an industrial breathing mask connected via tubing to the fungus farm. The tubes protruding from just below the goggles gave the bounty hunter an insect-like appearance. The two accordion tubes snaked over slender shoulders to the fungus farm within a large ruck-sack. It gave the bounty hunter a lumbering hunch-backed gait, but without that and the pair of high intensity light-filtering goggles one would be both blind and unable to breathe.

But the hunter had survived over an hour without gear once in order to subdue a bounty.

The hunter gazed through the dusty green goggles at a city far ahead, a thin horizontal sliver of scrap metal and tall, spidery rigging built into an elevated boulder fifty square hectares in size. The boulder looked as if an ancient god had balled up a massive clod of mud and then impaled it on a gargantuan tree stump and then much later a host of insects had taken up residence. The city sliced through the middle horizontally, sitting on a platform dotted with tall, ramshackle structures that ran from side to side. Several stair-steps of other lower layers descended to just above the desert floor. The hunter could just make out the lights of the refineries blinking in the distance and the rigging at the far north end of the structure, an arial dock for spacefaring ships and planetary transport that swarmed around it like bees.

The dust cloud near the bottom-most layer of platforms signaled that the welcoming committee was on its way, but the hunter did not slow, checking various firearms methodically and habitually. The wind picked up a bit, and with it roared ramshackle vehicles bouncing out of the dust, their riders hanging off the sides like broken fingers, each hanger-on gripping the roll-cage with one hand and the other brandishing either firearms or various sharp implements. The roar of cobbled together engines rose in volume, various alternate fuels propelling them across the sand. When they came within firing range they circled the bounty hunter, three of the vehicles kicking up sand in large rooster tails as they rotated around the lone figure. The rest came to a gravelly stop just twenty meters from the roaring ring before the wasteland daredevils faced the hunter with the grilles of their mutant-borne vehicles and the three taunting dune buggies finally came to a dusty, cloudy rest.

The bounty hunter stood quietly, gloved hands dangling, the many bands of what looked like long dirty strips of tattered canvas whipping about in the wind.

One of the welcoming committee, a large brute of a man without a shirt, his sore-pocked skin baked by the devilish heat of the desert, climbed out onto the rusting hood of his vehicle, his skull-like breathing mask hiding his apparent grisly features.

"Who you be?" came his raspy voice, a result of a lifetime of breathing recycled air. "What you want in Sanctum Mesa? You not visit, you pay travel tax. It be Mama Stone's law. She rule all wasteland soon. You see! We take Sanctum Mesa from Grand King Taharqua. We eat his fat flesh!"

The bounty hunter did not speak, did not move, save for a twitch of fingers.

A projectile weapon fired, and the bounty hunter felt the air disturb as a bullet zinged past an ear. The hunter knew who had fired it, but payed him no mind.

"You have free one," said the shirtless goon. "Next one pay with body juices. We scrape you off sand and eat what left!"

The brute made a wriggling gesture with fingers near his mouth to demonstrate the proposed cannibalism.

The wind blew a rogue gust just then, and the bounty hunter heard the faint click of a hammer cocking back. None of these troglodytes had energy weapons.

"Just passing through," came the hunter's low, computer-modulated voice. The mask amplified the sound of it, just enough to be low and intimidating, loud enough to be heard by all. "Now I don't have chids for a tax. But you're gonna let me pass anyway."

This comment brought about a sinister cackle of wasteland laughter from the welcoming party. A few of the cars revved their home-made engines, the distinctive whine of the superchargers echoing across the plain.

The bounty hunter's head swiveled slowly left to right then focused in on the leader who now bounded to the sand and strode, thick chest out like some albino ape, one hand reaching for his oversized side-arm.

"You roll dice, traveler," chortled the leprous wastelander. "Mama Stone have new plaything for games today. You 'member back this moment when you sit in cage rotting."

A shadow passed over the group then, and some of the wastelanders gazed upward, their pock-skinned hands trying to shield their weak eyes from the blazing twin suns.

The bounty hunter's head cocked to the side, then knees bent to crouch in the dust.

"I'm just here to collect is all. The rest of you can tear out of here."

A massive winged creature, its claws like silver razors and its long snout full of rows of jagged iron teeth saw the bounty hunter's signal and swooped out of the sky. In one rotating motion it made a bloody mess of five wastelanders including their shirtless leader. They didn't even have time to scream.

The rest did, however, and nervously pulled their projectile weapons, opening fire as the beast took to the air again. Its hide, covered with shiny metallic scales, made their projectile weapons obsolete. In response it dove down again with graceful undulation to slice into several more of their number. The bounty hunter took cover behind one of the blood-spattered vehicles, pulled a medium sized plasma rifle from the top of a rucksack, charged it with one pump, and then lay down a rapid-fire swath of energy that unleashed hell on twenty or so unsuspecting and poorly trained enemies.

Seconds passed as the drivers of the vehicles suddenly registered what was happening and kicked their engines into overdrive to flee. They spread out across the desert to either gain a more defensible position or to simply run away as fast as possible. As their rugged tires kicked up rooster-tails of sand, the long, quadrupedal beast landed near the bounty hunter and shook its angular head. Its metallic scales flexed and clicked, its vicious talons gripped the sand, and every surface reflected the blazing light of the twin suns. It tucked its razor wings in and gently licked the hand of the bounty hunter. At a silent command it gnashed its maw of needle teeth and turned to gobble a chunk of nearby wastelander meat. The bounty hunter knelt in the dust, picked up the severed head of the shirtless leader, and placed it in a duraplast bag produced from a rucksack.

"Good boy, Shytaar," said the hunter, approaching the beast and climbing onto its back. "Let's go collect our reward."

Shytaar unfurled his massive wings and with a whirl of dust the two were airborne, sailing toward the gigantic Sanctum Mesa in the distance, the light from the twin suns winking off of Shytaar's scales.

25

Guillermo managed to pull himself up off of the floor with Dervish's help. He took a second to stare through the porthole of the bulkhead where he saw a long hallway with a cracked door at the end of it where he had almost lost his life.

"Good job back there," he said to Dervish, looking her up and down. "You saved my life again."

Dervish raised her metal-enhanced arms in a display of thankfulness.

"It is the least I could do after I tried to kill you," she said. "I am forever —"

"Save it," Guillermo grunted. "You paid your debt, old girl. Now let's go see if we can find Mitsuki."

They strode forward, bouncing along, the anti-gravity generators still not working at full capacity. Guillermo here and there had to place his hand along the wall to steady himself. Soon they found a familiar corridor where Mitsuki waited, a warm smile greeting him. Adanez appeared behind her from a nearby doorway, but her expression was somewhat strained.

"Looks like we're back in the cross-rip again," said Adanez.

"Cross-rip?" Guillermo asked.

"She said it's a half-way point between two FTL destinations," offered Mitsuki. "Kind of like a limbo of sorts between destinations. We are somehow sitting in the middle of a stable wormhole."

"The ship is really old, Guillermo," Adanez said. "Some kind of glitch in the FTL software that was never fully scrubbed...the result of an experiment...or a miracle if you ask certain people. God knows I've tried. Without a complete overhaul or refit, for which we will never see the spare parts, we have probably another three or four jumps left. After that, the ship completely spins out of cross-rip and appears randomly in some corner of the universe. We are not sure where the end of the wormhole leads. Some think that its old Earth, but at least that's what is theorized."

Adanez waved her hand for them to follow her and they all proceeded down the corridor to an adjoining anteroom where a large plasteel porthole looked out on a strangely shimmering exterior. It looked to Guillermo like a broken mirror that reflected various points of light and dark, where colors blended and coalesced into a prismatic display. It was mesmerizing, a sight not for human eyes, something that both frightened and intrigued him at the same time. It was as if it were calling to him, pulling his mind down the darkness of the various alleyways of space-time.

"Beautiful, isn't it?" came a raspy voice beside him, and Guillermo turned to see a small woman dressed in a tattered brown robe, the frayed edges of which reached the rusting deck plating.

"I wouldn't say it was —" he began.

"Surely you understand the miracle that is taking place here," she said, her aged smile wrinkling the edges of her thin mouth. "God has provided a haven of rest as he says in his book...by his book."

A tall, dark skinned woman appeared suddenly in the doorway opposite them and then a crowd of children burst from around her legs, three of them no older than ten, as they pushed past the grimacing woman to nearly take Adanez out at the knees.

"Momma!" they shouted, and Adanez dropped to the metal floor to grab them up in a tight embrace, her hard features softened by a mother's tears. The other children found their respective parents and the reunions made Guillermo think about his own parents, lost so long ago to the organic in the Bug water supply.

"Oh my lovelies!" laughed Adanez, beaming. "You didn't give sister Ulah too much trouble, now did you?"

All of her children, two boys and one girl, suddenly grew quiet and nodded, their arms folded.

"We kept your precious ones safe while you were away, Clover," said the old woman, her kindly face cracking a smile. "But they were no trouble at all."

Adanez nodded at Ulah as she exited the room.

The elderly woman cleared her throat to speak and Adanez struggled past her kids to stand near her.

"I'm sorry, Guillermo," Adanez said, placing a hand on the old woman's shoulder. "This is Priestess Iona Jung. She is on the high council of the Shibboleth and our spiritual leader."

"Spiritual?" Guillermo scoffed. "You mean to tell me you believe in a higher power? A being of infinite power or whatever? Look around you, lady. There aren't any more —"

Guillermo was interrupted by a swift jab to the ribs by Mitzuki's elbow and Guillermo's gaze fell suddenly on the smallest of Adanez's three children, the little girl, who only stared at Guillermo in disbelief.

"Eden is real, sir," said the little waif. "You just have to believe."

"Have some respect, Guillermo," Mitsuki said. "These

people just saved our lives. Least you could do is not be a v'oshtu."

Guillermo shoved his hands into his pockets and turned to the old woman, bowing slightly at the waist.

"Forgive me, Priestess," he said wryly. "I won't make fun of your imaginary god again."

He then turned to the little girl and winked.

"And the old man who delivers presents probably knows how to travel through other-space and will be visiting you, too, little kid."

The old woman stepped between Guillermo and the little girl, her watery blue eyes staring intently, and she placed a crooked finger on the tip of Guillermo's nose before drawing back her hand.

"Your very presence is proof of this imaginary God you speak of," she said, her mouth drawn and grave. "For you and this girl are the key to bringing the AI to its knees, to helping us find our way back to Eden."

Guillermo pointed at the little girl.

"That girl?"

"No," Mitsuki said, clearing her throat. "I think she means me."

Mitsuki squinted one eye and scratched her head.

"So you mean… What could the two of us possibly do to defeat the AI? It does seem a little out there, if you ask me."

"Those Phaedrans from whom you just escaped," she explained. "Are the hunters sent out to find you, to find any Shibboleth colonies left in order to eradicate them. AI is hunting the coded children, the children we coded with the sacred text. You and this rude young man were the final hope, the ones we found on Phaedra Prime, before we had to spirit you away and hide you in the Five Rims. Today is a great day, children. Today God has brought you home to us so that we may finally complete the task that was planned so many years ago. We can finally go home."

Guillermo put his hands on his hips.

"Hold on a second," he said, his head tilting forward. "You said Eden. You mean Earth? That's a myth. If it exists, it's a burned out husk. Nothing would grow there. That's why we came here all those hundreds of years ago. How do you know it's habitable?"

Adanez's little girl strolled over quietly and gripped Guillermo's dangling fingers and he offered her a glance before turning his gaze back on the Priestess.

She only laughed.

"I have faith," she said with a smile, humored by the simple gesture of this child. "I have faith that it is there. We all do."

Suddenly the clawed hand of Dervish gripped Guillermo's shoulder, and he turned to face her, his face reflected in her compound eyes.

"You must be calm," Dervish said. "My senses tell me that this Terran believes this to be true. She is not lying to you. Her belief is strong."

Guillermo pulled her hand free, still allowing the little one to hold on to his metallic fingers.

"I don't care," he growled, looking down at the little girl who pulled away and was scooped up by Adanez. "My whole life I've survived because I know when something is a bad deal, and looking out this window I can tell this whole ship is sitting in the middle of one big bad deal. We have to get out of this FTL limbo."

The old woman stepped closer to him and Mitsuki only looked at the floor. The child let out a soft giggle at Guillermo and smiled, her two front teeth missing.

"We must find your third, Guillermo," said the old woman, her eyes filling with tears. "We must find her and bring her back. She left us a few years ago because the enemy had taken her daughter. She hunts for her now, but we believe we have located her and need your help to bring her back. When she comes back to us, is reunited with the two of you, she will understand her true purpose and will surely help us return to Eden. It is what you were created to do."

"There's a third?" Mitsuki asked.

"Yes," Adanez advanced, letting her daughter down and watching her join her brothers. "And she's more hostile toward our cause than the two of you combined."

26

The command shuttle emerged from the black orb of the wormhole like an obsidian arrowhead materializing from a gaping dirty wound. Its braking thrusters engaged and it rotated gracefully on its approach to the main hangar bay of the *Victorum*. It floated through the energy screen that contained the bay's stale atmosphere before descending to the deck where hundreds of Phaedran soldiers stood in long columns, rows deep and perfectly still. All soldiers stood eyes front, like columns of terra-cotta warriors standing silently, plasma rifles resting on their right shoulders.

Commander Deryn Ivory, Security Chief Absalom Liberty and Dr. Erasmus Spurling stood in a path between two large columns of soldiers as they faced the lowering landing ramp that dropped from the bottom of the now silent shuttle. When the clanking of boots on the landing ramp could be heard, Absalom waved his hand and the mass of soldiers, male and female, shouted a deep roar of welcome and then grew silent in unison.

Walking toward the Commander and her subordinates were two figures, one of them a young woman with dark hair who wore the signature cyber-armor of high command. The other, his body stooped like question mark, was the Conduit, Thorburn Plath. His black robes dragged behind him, his metallic lenses like a crude pair of binoculars replacing the flesh of his eyes. He moved closer, his claw-like hands curled at his waist, his pointy elbows protruding. He approached Commander Ivory and one gnarled finger touched her left collarbone. She immediately screamed and fell to the deck, writhing in searing pain. Small threads of blue electrical current flashed across her face and neck.

"The Shibboleth have eluded you again, Commander," he rasped. "Perhaps you are not worthy of command... much less the Divine Computat's holy augmentation."

"No, Conduit!" she gibbered. "I will — I will *remedy* the anomaly."

The Conduit flared out his crooked fingers and several metallic objects erupted from the commander's body, her second and third in command grinning as they were spattered with crimson. The landing bay grew silent save the echoing gasps of the commander's failing lungs.

"I now appoint you Commander of this ship, Absalom," said Plath, forming the augmentations into a messy magnetic ball before scattering them to the floor. "I am sure you will not fail the Divine Computat. Your war record is indeed impressive."

Absalom pounded a heavy fist into his open hand and bowed before the Conduit, dropping to one knee, and the doctor did the same, his eyes blinking erratically.

"I live to serve!" they shouted in unison.

Immediately the army around them shouted the same refrain, a mantra of loyalty, a sound that shook the deck plating.

"I live to serve! I live to serve! I live to serve!"

The Conduit placed gnarled hands on hips and scanned the troops, his neck craning forward like some cybernetic vulture.

"This loss is only a minor setback," he droned. "The reason the Shibboleth want these refugees will soon be determined, but we must convince them that our cause is more just. Once we are able to locate their base we will eradicate the anomaly completely. The Most High Computat will provide the means and the coding for our victory."

He raised his fists above his mottled head.

"The Most High Computat wills our service!" he cried.

A rumble was heard as the Phaedran troops stomped their armored feet.

"We live to serve! We live to serve! We live to serve!"

Conduit Plath looked down at his kneeling subordinates.

"Rise," he commanded, his aged voice modulated with mechanical augmentation. "Take me to my quarters immediately, and then we will begin to locate the anomalies."

Absalom and Spurling stood to their feet quickly, but Absalom moved to the side of the Conduit as if he had been there many times before, for he had history with the Conduit. They began to walk between the rows of soldiers as they approached the hangar doors. The doctor fell behind them, walking with his thin hands behind his back.

"Conduit," said Absalom, his eyes averted. "I was able to attach a tracer to the hull of the offending world ship before it jumped away to FTL. However, the tracer is producing an odd signal that is as if they are submerged in between destinations. Is this possible? What we understand of Neo-quantum physics is being tested..."

The old cybernetic Conduit managed a disturbing smile, more of a stretching of pale skin over glistening metal teeth.

"It is as I have suspected for some time," he wheezed. "They are trapped inside the wormhole...stuck somewhere between... which means their FTL drive is breathing its last. Unless we know the destination point, or the exact coordinates within the wormhole, we cannot hope to locate them. I am not sure how this limbo is possible, but it is the only plausibility. The Most High Computat will be pleased to learn of your tracker. We will utilize the great wisdom of the Computat for the calculations necessary to find and destroy them. I will see to your next augmentation myself for this, Commander."

"Thank you," said Absalom. "I live to serve."

"And now, take me to this bug queen you spoke of on your last communique, Doctor Spurling." said the Conduit. "She will unwittingly be the final piece to our securing the realm for the Most High Computat. We will reclaim what was once ours."

27

A rusty iron cage squatted empty on an anti-grav platform in the swirling dust of the wasteland. Heaped around the base of Sanctum Mesa were mounds of trash and waste fed by detritus and filth that rained and fluttered down from high above. Several groups of vile, grime-covered wastelanders rooted around in the steaming garbage.

A group of tattooed and pock-marked soldiers stood guard throughout the rabble, their home-made zip guns pointed at the stragglers whom they kicked or rifle-butted to an endless task of finding sustenance for the higher level dogs. The rummagers, covered in grime, rarely looked up from their labor. When they did it was with masks of wide eyed fear. They rasped and wheezed in the thin atmosphere, their yellowed eyes bulging.

A shining, glittering hulk approached, its low form skulking toward them. Riding atop the beast the lone bounty hunter had already raised a plasma rifle. The hunter's face, hidden behind amber goggles and battle-scarred breathing mask appeared a horrific specter emerging from the watery mirage of heat waves and reddish dust.

The guards turned abruptly, training their zip guns on the

stranger, and in seconds a duraplast bag was produced. With a flick of a wrist the contents were tossed to the baking sand where the severed head of Mama Stone's general bounced like a grisly ball of meat, the teeth clicking together as it rolled.

A rusting globe descended then, its repulsers whining, until it hovered just meters away from the stranger.

"State your business, traveler," it said, the voice inhuman, a low vibration and crackling with the static of worn sound emitters.

"I have audience with Papa Exu," said the bounty hunter, the voice modulated and mechanical. "He owes me some chids for removing this interloper and quelling the war between himself and Mama Stone. I imagine she's long gone by now."

The globe hovered over to the head which lay slack-jawed upon the sand, a clicking like that of a camera shutter was heard, and then the machine hovered back to the bounty hunter. A metallic release was heard and then the front panel of the squatty cage dropped to the ground with a harsh clang.

"Enter the conveyance," said the globe ascending quickly, its crackling voice trailing. "You will receive further instructions upon arrival. Leave the beast or you will be killed."

The bounty hunter adjusted a wide brim hat and followed the orb with a steady gaze before dismounting the creature with one motion and then patting its jagged snout with one gloved hand.

"It's ok, boy," the hunter said soothingly. "Just go hunt for a while and I'll call you."

Shytaar clicked his thick tongue in response and then blinked coldly. The sand swirled around them as the creature took to the air, its long armored wings flapping in slow, steady strokes.

Ragged strips of material fluttered about the bounty hunter's costume like soft-carbon tentacles in the fierce desert wind. Striding forward, the dead eyes of the beheaded general dumbly looking on, the bounty hunter powered up a plasma rifle when mounting the platform and did not flinch as the door to the cage rose, slamming shut behind.

Soon the repulsers warbled to life and it began to slowly ascend to the first level of the city. The hunter looked below and saw the wasteland guards fighting over the head, thinking absently that this might make for a good wager as to who would be the new majordomo for Mama Stone.

But the bounty hunter had bigger quarry.

The journey to the first level took very little time, but in that span the hunter thought about the child. The bounty hunter had followed many leads, most of them dead ends, in hopes of finding her, of finding her daughter. The trail had run to this cobbled together wasteland city far out on the outer rim of this system, a place called Exile, a place where the un-augmented were dumped like discarded bones. It had cost a well-fitted ship, all the resources she could muster, and one more power core to a plasma rifle completely spent after that last skirmish. She would not return to the Shibboleth. Their foolish crusade had cost too much of what she held dear.

Papa Exu, however, was one more link in the chain of clues to finding Grace.

The hunter's eyes closed, the image of her daughter's face floating there, so real but not real. The hunter would find Grace, call up the Shibboleth, and finally make peace with them. Cooperation would not be made with their unrealistic crusade, for she would continue on her way after that.

The cage stopped moving, and the opposite side dropped open with a metallic clang. Her eyes flicked open. Twenty or so guards, the business end of zip-guns pointed menacingly, stood in uneven rows. She stowed the plasma gun and raised both hands in a gesture of peace.

Maybe they won't know I'm out of juice.

Always carry backups.

This gesture did not satisfy the rabble who approached with much vigor, prodding her torso with their rifles and grunting in a strange mash of Terran. The dura-carbon weave didn't permit their rifle barrels to hurt her, but made it easy for her to slip through them and board another waiting cage suspended by a massive cable. The mass of armed grunts wore various scrap and strips of clothing, trussed with cords and strips of hide and chains. All weapons and armor were in multiple stages of disrepair and any exposed skin gave sign of the disease that many Terrans suffered here on this desolate world.

She entered the second cage, blankly turned to face the guards and then watched as the door slammed shut again. This time the cage rose more quickly. There was much further to go. Before the hunter could shift a foot, four Terrans, each with repulsor packs on their back, landed with a thud on top of the cage. The vessel rocked back and forth with their added weight as the new arrivals seemed more calm, their motions measured, not as spasmodic or savage as the ground dwellers.

She casually waved at these new guests.

"Hey, fellas. No harm done."

All ignored the bounty hunter save one, whose breath mask like the face of a praying mantis only stared blankly, studying the lone figure within the cage. The guard atop the cage rotated a large chamber inside his plasma rifle, like the revolver of a massive pistol, and then pulled a modified lever on the side of it. A shower of blue sparks rained down into the cage before he pointed the jury-rigged contraption in the bounty hunter's direction.

Muffled, giddy laughter could be heard all around the cage.

"Nice toys," she said.

Soon the cage shuddered to a stop and the front panel fell open on a platform pock-marked with rust and age. She emerged to a better welcome, and if not for a sensor package installed within the comm system, the four human hornets would not be heard landing behind with catlike grace. The eager one with the giddy laugh pressed his rifle to her back to gently nudge their guest forward.

A crowd of more sophisticated Terrans gathered here, their clothing more new and seemingly manufactured. There were rows of markets and outdoor barter booths, a vast bazaar where scavenged scrap metal, weapons and recycled foods were sold. The hunter paid no mind to it, even if slightly tempted to shop for yet another gadget, but for now the bargain must be made with Papa Exu. If success was managed with that particular underling perhaps the throne of Grand King Taharqua could be reached at last.

All in good time.

A new squad of soldiers approached, walking in lockstep with plasma rifles raised. In moments the hunter was surrounded, but the citizens of Sanctum Mesa's upper levels only looked on with bland curiosity before moving away. The reavers who had accompanied her thus far began to scatter before Taharqua's personal guard. Out of the crowd emerged a bald man wearing a baggy scarlet jump suit. A criss-cross of bandoliers carried large projectile cartridges. Cold eyes stared out over a breathing mask that hid his nose and mouth. Those dark eyes blinked in the double sunlight and his black skin shone with a health and vigor not gifted to many on this harsh world.

"Bounty hunter," came the basso voice of Papa Exu, amplified by his breathing apparatus. "You have brought the payment, then. Where's the head you promised?"

The soldiers parted as Papa Exu approached, stopping a safe six meters away from the bounty hunter.

"The job is done...left it at the gate to feed the dogs," she said, her true voice hidden by the vocalizer. "Now I expect to get what I want. I'm sure you saw it on your looking-scopes."

"You will be paid — " began Papa Exu.

"I desire audience with Grand King Taharqa."

At the mention of the warlord's name the crowd grew silent around them and all of the masked faces stared blankly.

"You have not earned the right to make demands of the Grand King," wheezed Papa Exu. "You will gain audience only if he wishes it. For now you will fulfill the other part of the bargain."

The hunter gripped tight the stock of the plasma rifle, hoping the bluff that it was fully charged held true.

"I never agreed to that part, Exu," she growled, the modulator taking on a throaty tone. "If you try to hold me to it I'm gone, and you can get someone else to do your dirty work. That raw-head I brought in for you isn't the only insurrectionist who wants the riches of this city. You'll soon have a war on your hands that you can't win. Mama Stone is just one of many pocket despots."

Papa Exu folded his thick arms in front of his chest and bellowed out a laugh, leaning into the force of it. The crowd began to thin out, many of them going behind the booths or vacating the area entirely. They were creatures of habit, and those who survived this place instinctually knew when their lives might be threatened by stray plasma fire.

"The balance of Grand King Taharqa's kingdom is kept in check by fear," said Papa Exu, nodding his head. "That and the understanding that the wastelanders will always thirst, an understanding that we are the source for all water and clean oh-two. The majority must make room for the comfort of the minority. It is the price they pay for living in their caste."

"I have news for you, Exu," the bounty hunter said flatly. "Your peasant class is figuring out how to get their own water and fresh air. Soon you will be in a war of attrition like you've never experienced."

"You lie!" hissed Papa Exu. "What proof do you have?"

She shook her rifle at him.

"I won't waste breath on a lackey! What I have to say is only for the King...if he has enough chits to pay for it. I got the info for their bases and defenses right here in my noggin. I suppose King Taharqua would like that knowing. What say you?"

At this, the soldiers closed in, their plasma rifles equipped with stun rods which now struck at the bounty hunter, but the electricity arced around in a bubble, feeding back to their rifles and causing each to deactivate with a popping sound and a puff of black smoke.

"I suggest you take me to that bloated king of yours," she said. "This is the last time I will say it."

Papa Exu touched the side of his mask, and the bounty hunter knew that a communication was being received. In moments the hunter was being led away to a vast staircase built from various scraps of discarded space craft. She saw stabilizer wings, old cockpit canopies and rusty deck plating all haphazardly welded together.

She knew her quest was nearing an end, and the top of those stairs was the doorway.

Wordlessly, they began the long climb to the throne room.

28

Guillermo, Mitsuki and Dervish followed Priestess Iona Jung through a few corridors until they emerged in a massive hydroponics bay. Centuries ago it housed enough greenery to supply food for the Terran's long journey from their resource depleted system to the Five Rims. Now it was rusted and grimy, only a few rows of plants growing in a dimly lit environment which felt stale and smelled of mold and decaying fruit. Several of the solar radiation replicators far above either flickered or were broken, but enough stayed on to give light to the remaining plants.

One large tree grew from the artificial soil in the center of the bay, and the group sat beneath it in a few mismatched metal chairs scattered about. Dervish sat on the patchy grass at the base of the tree.

"So tell me about this third person," Guillermo began. "And what she has to do with us."

Iona Jung, priestess of The Way, settled into one of the chairs and shifted her small frame, her old bones aching with the ravages of age. She produced a small device, a medical scanner with several modified wires and strange bits of metal protruding from it, and then switched it on. It hummed pleasantly as she pointed it at Mitsuki and then Guillermo.

"Ah yes," she said with a thin smile. "It is as we thought. The DNA coding is still intact. Each of you carries one third of the code. As soon as we can convince Aura to join us, then we can begin our assault. You can help us find her, yes?"

"You didn't really answer my question," said Guillermo. "What does she...Aura, I guess... have to do with us?"

The old woman shifted in her chair again, crossed her thin ankles and smiled. Adanez's three children stumbled into the hydroponics bay laughing and chasing one another. They ran toward the tree, but when they saw the Pristess they stopped, gave her mischievous smiles and then darted away through a grove of low plum trees. Soon all that could be noticed of them was their tinkling laughter some distance away.

Priestess Iona took in a breath and then let it out slowly.

"The three of you hold the code that will destroy the AI. It will free our people from its control and will allow you to theoretically control the AI's matrix that boosts FTL travel. Once the code was discovered within the text, it was determined that the only way to keep it safe was to encode it on the DNA of you three special children. We then decided to scatter you throughout the Five Rims to ensure your safety."

"Why not just put it on a device or store it elsewhere?" Mitsuki asked. "Why us?"

The old woman chuckled.

"Because the code must be combined with a living being in order to interface with the AI. Living beings like you who have been augmented from birth."

"I have been augmented?" Mitsuki said, eyes wide. "How?"

"We stole the three of you from Phaedra Prime when you were babies. You, Mitsuki, survived a hostile jungle on Ontocca, am I right? And Guillermo, you were unable to accept the regeneration process for your missing arm. Aura, the one we call the bounty hunter, also has special talents. It is what makes the three of you unique. The AI has been looking for you ever since, and they nearly had you. You see, you are a Phaedran experiment."

"Experiment for what?" Guillermo said, leaning forward in his chair.

"The AI wants to create perfect Terrans, Terrans DNA coded with subservient natures. It wants to control everything, to perfect the Terran race or any race who opposes it. Ultimately it has designs on the entire known universe. We stole you away, with much sacrifice no less, to use you against the AI. You see, we found a code within the text to override the AI's mind."

Guillermo reached out, took Mitsuki's hand, and she looked at him, her face a puzzle of emotion.

"So this text," he said, turning back to the Priestess. "What is it?"

"When it is needed most," said Iona, her eyes welling up with tears. "This text has proven the existence of God by its own revelation. Within the text, the ancient Bible, there exists a code hidden in the ancient languages that when sequenced into DNA can overwhelm and destroy the mind of the AI."

Guillermo erupted into a fit of laughter, his voice echoing in the stillness of the hydroponics bay. Mitsuki stared at the patchy grass growing on the floor. Dervish stood and leaned against the trunk of the tree.

"You people are *ch-u-ku-trar*!" Guillermo said, standing to his feet and pointing an accusing finger at the Priestess. "You mean to tell me you think some ancient mythological god gave you the code to stop the AI? Prove it. I've been through a lot of chert, lady. Putting my hopes in some mythological, all knowing being is beyond my mental capacity...much less my patience."

"And he doesn't have a lot of that either," Dervish offered.

Iona's face was drawn, her eyes narrowing. She took in a deep, patient breath and then let it out.

"It is a matter of faith, Guillermo, like many other things. We know this will work because we were given certain assurances. You see...it has worked before."

Guillermo opened his mouth to speak, but fell silent. His gaze fell on Mitsuki, and in her eyes saw the signal to respect Iona's beliefs. Beyond this, when he looked back at Iona, the old woman's gaze was one of disappointment and true pain. They sat in silence for a time, and Guillermo opened his mouth to speak, but Dervish cut him off.

"Worked before? Tell me of this."

Guillermo looked at Dervish and cleared his throat, and the old woman leaned forward somewhat painfully in her chair.

"We are sitting in this FTL limbo space because of the code," she said. "We fed it into the FTL drive computer, nearly a century ago, and it brought us here. All that we know about FTL physics tells us that we should not exist in this dimension. We should have suffered catastrophic failure of the FTL drive, phase shifted through a planet or a star, or been pulled into a quantum singularity. Our presence here defies all knowledge of FTL travel. We are currently existing outside of space-time, somewhere in a quantum pocket if you will. As far as we can tell, this place where we reside should not exist."

Guillermo stroked his chin.

"Yeah, I'll give you that," he said. "It's a difficult dance the FTL drives are doing to keep us here for sure...and I'm not really sure how. But the fact that you can't do many more jumps out is proof that this is not natural at all, regardless of how you bend space-time. But that doesn't mean some ancient god of old Earth is doing it. It's just a strange and unexplainable event. Those things happen all the time.

Doesn't mean it's god."

Dervish stood, paced back and forth on the patchy grass in front of them, and then turned to face Iona.

"Before the war the Queen had placed me in charge of the FTL project deep beneath Royal City. I was privy to all information regarding the newest technology, but a ship of this size lodged within FTL between destinations is indeed impossible. It is beyond my understanding of space-time. Have you determined where this wormhole leads? Where it might eject the ship at the end?"

"Adanez has made more progress than any other," Iona offered. "And she seems to think...to believe... that the wormhole is one that stretches farther than any other wormhole created thus far. She believes, with sufficient calculations and power our engines do not have, that it will deposit us in Eden...old Earth."

"Impossible as that sounds," Mitsuki said suddenly, breaking her silence. "It is an intriguing theory. What is sustaining this wormhole? Usually there is a quantum ignition point and a terminus. As far as I can tell from what I saw in the engine room this wormhole is not sustained by anything at all. I can't explain it."

"Neither could we," Iona explained. "We are supposed to travel to the end of it, I know, but we have not sufficient power to do so. Our hope is that the three of you will be able to utilize whatever abilities you have to get us there."

"You have a lot of faith in us, then," Guillermo said quietly. "But I just think you are living in a dream world."

"It is something we take on faith, Guillermo," Iona said, her voice a deep sigh. "It is my hope that you will join me in this belief."

They all stared at the ground, the patchy grass and dying leaves of the tree a reminder of time running out for them even though currently they existed outside of it. Iona reached out and took Guillermo's metal hand in hers and he did not pull away. He sat next to Mitsuki.

"We are able to exit this limbo at will, with much strain on the engines no less," she explained. "How we appear at the right time however is still a mystery. We just plug in where we want to go and pray. However, we know for certain that we only have a few jumps left in the engines, at least this is according to Adanez. We need to plan our next moves carefully. We have located the third child...who is currently on Exile, a world where the Phaedrans send their augmentation candidates who are not able to bond...or those who refuse."

"This third person," Guillermo asked. "Are they my brother or sister? And is Mitsuki my sister?"

"No," said Iona. "You are all three...unique...with DNA that allows your chromosomes to act as storage devices for the code. It seems that you were conceived by Terrans but then your DNA was...as far as we can understand... reconstructed somehow."

Guillermo let out a long sigh.

"So we aren't brother and sister."

"No," Iona blinked. "You are not."

"Oh that's good," he said, a slight chuckle as he looked at Mitsuki who only offered an uncomfortable smile. "Cause all this stress makes me do things like this."

He pulled Mitsuki to him and kissed her. She didn't pull away.

"It is good that you two have bonded," said Iona with a wry smile, watching the two of them with a smile. "Perhaps the third will cooperate, but she feels that we betrayed her somehow. The enemy has warped her mind through deception and lies. She seeks her child even though we told her it would be too much of a risk to our cause. She cares not for us, but you must convince her otherwise."

"A mother will guard her young," Dervish offered.

"Look," Guillermo said, looking to Mitsuki for support. "I'll help you find this... Aura... I guess. She sounds like someone we could use in a fight. But we've got to work on the plan to take down the AI. Mystical magic just isn't my thing."

Footsteps were heard, and Adanez approached through a nearby bulkhead door that slid creakily aside. She wiped her greasy hands with an equally greasy rag. Her kids peeked out from behind a plum bush, giggled, and she waved at them.

"We are ready for the jump to Exile, Iona," Adanez said. "We can't do this too many more times, but this is indeed necessary. Guillermo and Mitsuki should ready themselves for transport. The shuttle we stole is not much of a ship, but I'm sure I can pilot it safely down to Exile."

"Transport?" asked Guillermo. "Did you fix the guns on that thing?"

Adanez only tilted her head and looked sidelong at him.

"Uh, yeah," she said. "Added a few surprises, too. This place is one of the most dangerous in this sector. I'd rather go to Phaedra Prime than Exile."

Mitsuki stood and Guillermo started from his chair.

"Point me to the ship."

29

The grand staircase of Sanctum Mesa was a patchwork of hull plating and architecture of a by-gone star-faring era. The bounty hunter climbed it steadily, each step guarded by the watchful eye of the masked and armored city guards, their plasma rifles raised and ready for use.

She paid them no mind.

Inside heavy goggles a map overlay of the city was visible to her in green lines, and Shytaar's homing signature could be seen hovering nearby, far overhead.

At the top of the grand staircase an immense court level spread out in several hundred square meters. In the center the Grand King Taharqua sat upon a throne of platinum plated metal, his obese girth shaded from the harsh sun by a tattered and oily canopy that spread the full length and width of the platform. He was surrounded by attendants, a harem of women lying at his dropsied, purple-toed feet, and a host of personal guards, all of them arrayed in a varied patchwork of handmade armors and weapons.

A gaggle of filthy children wearing ornate and bulky vests squatted before the throne, their dull eyes staring at the bounty hunter, their little mouths curled in wicked smirks.

The Shibboleth Code

The king was nearly nude save a ragged cloth that hung down between his blubbery legs. His eyes were hidden behind a set of black goggles that seemed to have set themselves in the flabby flesh of his face. Fat lips peeled back to reveal a yellowing graveyard of teeth, and he hissed loudly into a device floating near his face which amplified his voice for the court.

"They say you kill Aartok, that Mama Stone general. Wastelander uprising stopped?" said the King, a string of drool pouring from his lips. It was quickly wiped away by a tremulous harem girl.

The bounty hunter stopped, bowed at the waist, then slung the plasma rifle. The guards flinched, but one wave from the king's pudgy hand and they fell back obediently. The fact that she could still brandish weapons in the King's presence was either due to arrogance or outright sun-burned stupidity.

"I left the severed head of your enemy at the gate," she said through a vocal enhancer. "I have dispatched the rebel general as requested, and now you pay up. Now you give me back what is mine."

A deep, wheezy laugh echoed around the court as the corpulent king chuckled menacingly. A few of the harem girls uttered nervous giggles.

"Yes," said the King. "In time. I need more favor."

The bounty hunter hissed out a growling vocalization from the breath mask.

"I refuse to do anything else until you bring me what you took from me. If harm has come to…"

"Possession safe, bounty hunter," came the low voice of the King. "In safe place with guards on watch night and day."

With deliberate motion the bounty hunter reached up and slowly pulled the breathing mask and goggles away. Standing before the king was a Terran female, her bright red hair clinging to her sweat-stained face, her pale skin glistening, her deep green eyes flitting about the crowd.

"You regret taking that off, bounty hunter," the King said, his harem girls scurrying around behind him.

"I wanted you to look directly into my eyes, King," wheezed the woman, coughing once, her eyes like two green flames. "To see the face of the one who will end you if you don't do what you promised."

A low rumbling laugh escaped the King's fat lips as he showed her his yellowed and rotting teeth.

"If I make you do jobs," he said. "I keep little girl forever. You be my slave like all rest."

A millisecond barely passed before the plasma rifle was in her hands, and she pointed it directly at the fat King's bloated head.

"Give me the girl or…"

The king raised a plump finger.

"Ahh. If weapon fires, then child is harmed. This is deal."

A sudden hot wind blew across the platform then, and the woman stared at the King wide eyed. Bits of sand blew into them, but she didn't blink, her force of will stronger than the urge to clear her vision. She could see the King and his entourage, knew how many guards surrounded her from the sides and from behind, had counted them on the way in. She weighed her options, looked at the children, and slung the rifle again.

The King made another motion with one chunky hand.

There was a rumble of voices, and then she was being attacked, but her reflexes were greater than theirs. She was grabbed by a large guard to her left and then used the momentum of the guard against him to fall back and blast a hole in his head with a hidden plasma pistol ejected from her sleeve. She rolled, used another guard as a shield as she took down two more, her face a blank mask of concentration. The harem girls moved to shield the King with their bodies as the little children rushed forward and surrounded the bounty hunter, their little hands locking in a soft embrace, and then the guttural voice of the King could be heard in the dank air.

"My children loyal," he said. "Vests laced with boom-clay. If you not stop you splatter…take them with you. I get new slaves."

She looked down at the child in front of her, saw the wry smirk there, and through the grime recognized the face of her daughter. A thought came to her to grab her child, run to the edge of the platform and leap with her, hope that Shytaar could catch them, but the thought faded as soon as it had materialized.

The vest would surely be detonated.

Instead she dropped her weapon to the floor and knelt just as seven guards rushed forward and pinned her to the hard rusty metal. After a harsh beating which she thought she might not survive, she found herself in a metal cage suspended beneath the lower platform of the city, with a view of the desert floor several hundred meters below.

30

The modified transport freighter dropped through the atmosphere of Exile, its four black tapered wings sending swirls of upper atmosphere dust in its wake. Its rounded, blunt nose punched through the low lying thin layer of smog and descended toward the elevated junker city in the distance.

Sanctum Mesa was quick to respond over the comm.

"Ugly old freighter," rasped a wheezy voice. "Tell us what you want or become scrap metal."

A metallic hand waved over a set of controls.

"Transport seven-seven-two out of Phaedra Prime requesting immediate repairs and re-supply. We are also carrying a gift for his highness."

Silence save only the crackle of static.

"King not expecting pretty shiny," said the raspy voice, uttering a slight cough at the end of the sentence. "No more refugee from Prime planet, either. King's orders. Embargo."

"This pilot is assured the King will enjoy his new pet," said Guillermo. "It is a creature discovered on the far edge of known space. Something for the arena."

"No refugee?"

"No refugee."

More silence while the crew of the freighter held their breath, watching the elevated city grow ever closer, its rusty spires like the needles of a gigantic, beached sea urchin.

There was a faint sound of a microphone feeding back followed by a soft thump.

"Approach slip two-three-two at forty degrees, seven above azimuth," growled another voice. "A crew of cargo slaves will unload the gift."

"Thank you, Exile," said the pilot. "We appreciate your generosity, and hope to do business with you in the future."

The microphone had gone dead.

Guillermo turned to Mitsuki, Adanez and Dervish.

"I sure hope this works," he said. "If not, maybe the King won't eat us right away."

Mitsuki offered a strained smile.

"Couldn't be worse than that whiptail lair back on Ontocca, right?"

"It could," muttered Adanez. "This is Exile. It's where the Phaedrans throw all of their undesirables. These are the Terrans who were not able to bond with their nanotech and subsequently with the AI. Or they chose not to."

They settled back in their co-pilot chairs as they approached the tall spire that was slip two-three-two. Even from this distance they could see the gaggle of tattered peasants manning a large crank on the platform, causing it to extend slowly outward with much sweat and back-breaking effort. The platform lengthened shakily, jittering in the desert wind like a fragile blade of grass.

Guillermo spun the ship around to connect the rear coupler to the platform and then set the parking repulsers to hover hundreds of meters above the garbage-littered desert floor. Dervish slunk away, climbing into one of the maintenance hatches as planned while the three Terrans opened the aft cargo door. As the door slowly dropped, letting in blinding light from the unforgiving dual stars, they could make out the shabby form of a tall, thin Terran wearing a goggled breath mask that pulsated with cobbled together oxygen reclaimer technology.

"The world ship is still in orbit, right?" whispered Mitsuki out of the side of her mouth as she produced a respirator.

Guillermo nodded, donning his own breathing mask.

"As far as I know —"

Guillermo stomped down the ramp, extending a hand toward the shabby Terran.

"Hello! I suppose you are Janus?....Janus?...No?...Well, no matter."

He pointed at a large crate sitting inside the cargo bay of the ship behind him.

"We have to get this creature to the arena immediately or we fear we won't make our other shipment in time."

The shabby Terran took one look over its shoulder, and when he did the hangar slaves scurried out of sight, keeping their heads bowed low. The Terran turned around and took one step toward Guillermo, moving so close that his mask nearly touched Guillermo's.

"We get no messenger about gift," he rasped, and Guillermo recognized the voice as the second one he had heard over the comm. "Are you trying to wink our king? Many Phaedrans try to mulch him. All get winked instead."

The shabby one waved a hand and suddenly a rumble was heard as a horde of repulser-pack-wearing, breathing-masked, armed guards dropped onto the platform from above.

"Well," Mitsuki said. "That was unexpected."

"Shhhh." Guillermo said.

"We inspect cargo," said the shabby emissary. "You get much chits if you good, not try wink us."

Guillermo let out a nervous laugh.

"Nobody's trying to wink anybody around here," he said, turning to Mitsuki and Adanez. "You trying to wink anybody?"

"Nope," said Adanez.

"You?" asked Guillermo.

"No way," said Mitsuki putting up her hands, blinking her eyes against the dusty wind. "No winking. I can't even wink."

Guillermo smiled at the emissary and looked around at the mechanical flying monkeys.

"Y'see? No winking...and what do we call you?"

"I am Ripper," said the figure behind the mask. "I serve King."

"I bet you are," said Guillermo. "You look like a ripper. Well, get on with the inspection so we can leave. As I said, I have another shipment to deliver."

Four of the jet-pack-wearing goons shuffled forward, one of them with a slight limp, and they surrounded the large crate as Guillermo and crew stood to the side, their hands hanging at their sides. One of the goons produced a small hand-held scanner and began to take a few readings, a device cobbled together from several other devices. From the sparks it emitted Guillermo wondered if it might catch fire in the goon's gloved hand.

The scanning goon turned and muttered something to Ripper and soon they were all being taken at gunpoint to a waiting repulser elevator that dropped them a few stories to the main city platform. They walked calmly along, each of them knowing that the plan required that they play the King's games. Guillermo, however, decided to make small talk.

"So any idea how long this will take, Ripper? I mean, I really have a quota to meet. If people could grow FTL parts out of the ground I don't suppose they'd need my delivery service."

Ripper didn't speak and neither did the goons, just a grunt now and then as they climbed a series of steps to a massive throne room where the bloated King Taharqua sat surrounded by thinly dressed harem girls and several dirty children wearing strange bulky vests.

The Great Taharqua was snoring loudly.

"My lord," said Ripper in a moderately audible voice, startling Taharqua awake. "These merchants have slogged a beast for the arena, to give you much fun times."

The expression of surprise washed across the King's pock-marked face like a quick-moving aircraft shadow and was replaced with a glowering, frowning expression that did not give the trio much hope in completing the mission successfully.

"I not ordered any pets," growled the morbidly obese king. "Who send gift to majesty?"

Adanez dropped something out of her sleeve and into her hand, then looked at Guillermo, her eyes darting back and forth to signal him. Guillermo realized suddenly that he had not thought this far into the plan, remembering that he had sold his companions on dropping deep into this bottomless well of danger with the words "Don't worry. I have it all figured out." He randomly thought about Adanez's kids, the face of that little girl especially, and reasoned that he couldn't let Adanez get herself dead.

"I promised the lady I wouldn't tell," said Guillermo waving a few fingers at Adanez to signal her to put whatever weapon she was holding away. "I swore I wouldn't tell. Really, I did. But, oh king, you have a secret admirer and that secret admirer would rather not let her identity be known to you."

Silence except for the hot, dry wind.

Suddenly a rumbling, wheezing laugh could be heard from a vocalizer device that amplified the King's voice and allowed him to breathe a modicum of clean air.

"Clever one," said the King. "It thinks it get wink on King Taharqua."

"What is with this winking business?" Mitsuki blurted.

"Closed mouths!" screamed Taharqua. "What say this... admirer?"

Guillermo, surprised the King's vocabulary contained that word, continued.

"I'm sure in your great wisdom you have heard of Queen Shannon of the high desert?"

A murmur of voices echoed across the throne platform.

"I know of this person," warbled the King. "You say she is changing her mind?"

Guillermo laughed, jerking a thumb over his shoulder.

"That three kiloton beast in my hold is proof. Now if you'll just allow us to unload her, we'll be on our way."

The king rolled forward in his seat, and Guillermo was now surprised by the unusual mobility of such a rotund Terran.

"It will deliver beast to arena," said the King. "And then it will go."

The three of them began to back away, bowing at the waist, and Guillermo gave the others a wink.

Adanez and Mitsuki only smiled beneath their masks.

31

The three of them walked briskly back to the freighter. The two women trained their eyes forward, but Guillermo stared intently over his shoulder now and again.

He spoke into his wrist, and a tiny green holo-image of Dervish appeared to float above his forearm.

"You find this Aura or whatever her name is?"

"I have," crackled Dervish. "But you will not be pleased to know where she is located."

Guillermo gritted his teeth.

"Don't really care where she's located, Dervish. Just want to know if you can get her out of there. We have to unload our cargo and be skids up in a few minutes, and I want to know if we can get to her."

"There is another problem," said Dervish.

"No," Guillermo replied. "We can't have another one. We are full up for today."

"It is a problem, Guillermo," she replied, her tone incapable of showing emotion. "I cannot help that this is…"

"What is it?"

"It is Aura's daughter," Dervish explained. "She is with the Terran king, and she is wearing an explosive device."

"You mean to tell me..."

The trio passed some guards then, and Guillermo lowered his arm and smiled. As soon as they passed he was back to the conversation.

"You mean to tell me that little girl was sitting somewhere near the throne of that blob and we didn't know it?"

"Yes."

"Ok, so what else should I know?"

"Aura is being held in the staging area for the arena, Guillermo. I do not think it would be wise to extract her as yet. I believe I can find a way to extract the daughter, but I will need time."

"Chert," he said. "So what's the situation with getting Aura out?"

"There are a host of Taharqua's reavers near the arena. These are Terrans who have taken great pains to augment themselves mechanically even though they do not possess the genetic proclivity. It has turned them feral. It is quite..."

"I don't give a chert what's guarding her. I asked if we could get her out."

"At this point we are powerless."

"And what about the daughter?"

"They remove the children to feed them daily. I will not fail you."

"We can't risk the girl," Guillermo said. "But we have to get Aura out, and I'm sure she can help us get her daughter once we do. Don't do anything irrational."

"Guillermo, I am incapable of..."

"You know what I mean," Guillermo said, tightening his lips. "I'll get back to you."

He lowered his arm again to his side and sprinted ahead to join Mitsuki and Adanez, and when they reached the cargo ship and were safely inside, Adanez grabbed Guillermo by the metal arm.

"Guillermo," she said, her face flushed. "What is the plan here? Do you even have a plan at all?"

Guillermo laughed.

"Look, lady," he said. "I am in up to my eyeballs in wasteland mutie goodness out there, and I suppose I've come this far, and we've stuck our neck out for plenty of good causes. I'm in it till the end. But there's more at stake than just us. It's not just about Aura. There's a little girl out there wearing a bomb for a jumpsuit who needs our help and I haven't the foggiest idea of how to save her."

"We have to save them both," said Adanez, her arms folding across her chest. "We do not have the luxury of time, however. It is my duty to remind you that our world ship is parked just outside orbit of Exile, and if the Phaedrans show up to attack us the Shibboleth may not survive the jump back to FTL limbo. My kids won't survive the jump. They have to survive, Guillermo, regardless of my life. We have to get into that arena to rescue Aura, and we have to have a solid plan to do that."

Mitsuki placed a hand on her shoulder.

"You'll learn pretty quick that Guillermo usually has luck on his side. Of course we'll help you see this through. What about the cargo? We can unload it early, and while they are dealing with that we can get in through the confusion and get them out."

Guillermo walked away, approaching the back cargo ramp with fists balled up at his sides.

"You understand what we have to do, Mitsuki, and for that I admire you," said Adanez. "But Guillermo doesn't seem to know what is at stake here…"

Guillermo spun around.

"Don't know what's at stake?" He growled. "Of course I do! I just want to make sure everybody makes it out of here alive…or at least with most of their limbs. Your kids are what

I'm thinking about...and Aura's kid. We are headed into something that may be the end of us all, but your kids deserve their mom. Aura's kid deserves her mom. You need to get back to them, and I'm pretty sure that Aura would give her life to see her daughter escape. Right now I don't care whether the three chosen ones do our prophesied task and take out the AI. Right now all I can think about are the kids, and I'll give my life to see them to a safe place."

Adanez took three steps to the cargo bay control panel.

"I know what's at stake," she said, tears forming in her eyes. "I think about it every time I head out the door to another mission. My kids deserve the best.

She pointed at the crate.

"That will be the diversion we need to get this done," she said. "Let's stick to the original plan."

"Adanez," Guillermo said, his eyebrows furrowing. "The new wrinkle is Aura's daughter. We set off that EMP her vest might go off. Are you willing to take that chance?"

Adanez folded her arms, her eyes a smoldering fire. Guillermo placed a consoling hand on her shoulder.

"Let me do what I do best."

"And what is that?" asked Adanez, glaring at him.

"Throwing a breaker bar into the cogs of the machine," said Mitsuki. "Yeah, he's good at that."

Guillermo slowly eyed his companions, the wheels turning within his head, and his expression became grave.

"I have a plan and you're not going to like it," he said solemnly. "But I'm pretty sure it might work. Mind you, we might all die anyway. I've been practicing some new tricks, though, so we'll see."

32

Dana Adanez turned a small metal wrench over and over in her small hands, thinking of her mother, always thinking of her mother. She knew that her mother was someone important, that she was supposed to fix the ship when it broke down, but right now she was too concerned with finding her two brothers who had wandered away from her again.

The boys were always finding ways of leaving her out.

Ulah, her nanny, let them wander the ship pretty freely but today little Dana felt like there were a lot more crews working on damaged sections than usual. She was only halfway looking for her brothers, mostly out of concern but partly out of fear of losing them. She endured their taunting, but was always looking for a way to fit in with them. Even though she had witnessed much death in her short life, her father being taken only months before her birth, she tried not to let that worry her so much.

It had become routine.

She always heard about the bad Terrans who didn't like her family or her friends, and even though the adults in her life tried to explain them to her, she didn't really understand their hatred.

She knew how to get to the hydroponics bay, so she skipped along, finding the faded green line that led her to it. It was much lighter than it had been centuries ago, and there were many blots of rust along the way, but she found it easy enough.

She had lived on this ship all of her short five years.

The hydroponics bay was her favorite place. She could play here all day if mean old Ulah didn't make her study math and reading. Sometimes she would hide here among the rows of green corn stalks planted in the thin black synthesoil. She darted across the patchy grass and danced between the rows on her way to the outside plasteel wall where she sat with her bare feet propped up on the transparent steel window. Below her she could see the rust-brown planet where she was told her mother had gone.

Ulah had pointed it out yesterday when Dana wouldn't stop crying.

Dana thought it was strangely pretty even though she could tell from the way the adults made their faces that it was a bad place. She worried about her mother and wondered if she would be on one of those long journeys again. She plucked a leaf from one of the corn stalks and started to tear it into small strips that she then lay between her knees on the synthesoil.

Pretty soon she was weaving them together, telling herself that she was making it for her mother, and wondering if she would even notice this time.

And then she saw movement.

Something was moving along the outside of the plasteel window like a large spider, and in the faint glow of the hydroponic artificial sun she could see a slight glint of metal. She could hear the skrit-skrit-skrit of claws clinging to the uneven surface of the plasteel, and it was moving toward her from far above.

She scooted back, tried to rise to her feet, then stumbled backward. The thing was crawling ever quickly down the canopy toward her. The sound of its claws on the plasteel echoed in the large and vacant hydroponics bay.

She cried out, but no one came.

So she scooted back, her breath heaving in and out rapidly as she crawled backward, trying to hide behind the stalks of corn. But it was getting closer, and she could see two blue glowing eyes in the darkness on the outside of the habitat. It was staring right at her, grinning with bare skeletal teeth.

"Ulah!" she screamed, and the noise she made seemed to excite it as it began to claw at the outside of the hull, and she could hear the plasteel pop and groan in a threat to fail. The unmistakable sound of a vacuum pulling at the outside of the ancient plasteel was something from her nightmares, from every child's nightmares who dwelled in this broken-down world ship.

Suddenly someone grabbed at her, but she clawed at them and screamed as they pulled her away from the window. She beat at them with her little fists and screamed some more until she smelled the familiar smell of Ulah who was carrying her away from the monster on the other side of the plasteel. Ulah carried her through the rank and file of five Shibboleth soldiers who were now aiming their plasma rifles at the glass, each of them wearing environmental suits with helmets firmly attached.

As the bulkhead door closed behind her she was carried down the corridor, her arms and legs flailing. She heard the soldiers talking to one another about the automata on the outside of the hull, about how it had called home, and about how they only had a little bit of time left.

The bad Terrans were coming.

33

The arena was a large dome constructed from an assortment of rusted metal and shards of jagged durasteel plating from many hundreds of crashed starships. It hung from the lower platform of the city like the forgotten nest of some gargantuan bird of prey. The crowds of city dwellers, at least those of high enough favor or with enough resources to trade, were beginning to fill the makeshift benches in the caged gallery. They were of all walks of life, most of them dragging their weaponry with them. Here and there fights broke out over seating and position.

No one broke up the fights, for it had become tradition to spill blood before the main event.

On the end of the arena opposite the main entrance a large series of honeycombed cages held the forty or so prisoners who would be offered to the horrors awaiting them in the arena. Thousands of screaming wastelanders would soon be appeased by an annual gruesome show of violence, a tradition started by the Phaedrans during the reign of the Empire, but now a mutated devolution of what was once an organized show of flashy yet systematic execution.

Crawling along the outside of the prison cages were the

reavers, more machine than Terran, their crude robotic limbs and appendages clicking and scraping against the metal as they climbed around like anthropomorphic spiders on a large webwork of randomly welded metal bars and patternless cages. A hover skiff approached the arena slowly, the throne of King Taharqua visible to the gathering crowd. His bulk was surrounded by the bodies of his harem girls and small children wearing their explosive vests, one of whom was Aura's brainwashed daughter. Many had attempted to assassinate the king in the past, but they had all failed, every time killing an innocent shield of flesh instead.

The King's skiff docked with the uppermost level of the gallery, nearly seventy meters above the killing floor, and his majesty's subjects screamed and called to him, their cries like the sound of some unimaginable gaggle of demons hoping to gain favor from their wicked lord. A klaxon sounded, the grating honk of an ancient electronic horn, and soon a platform rose out of the middle of the arena upon which Papa Nexu stood, his voice bellowing over the roar of the gathering crowd.

"Welcome to the show, city folk!" he shouted, his gravelly voice amplified by an array of sound emitters. "Today you get to eat and get to breathe some of King Taharqua's air! Thank the great Taharqua, for your lives depend on his mercy!"

Rising out of the arena were several hover-skiffs loaded with canisters of clean air, and soon a host of raggedy servants were tossing them into the crowd. The possession of these rusty canisters was the object of great desire as the gaggle of city dwellers fought to grasp at them, some of them using the canisters to beat their neighbors to death for the chance at a fresh supply of clean oxygen mined from ancient ice deep beneath the planet.

After some time the crowd was appeased, their "bread"

distributed, and now the circus would begin.

Papa Nexu, standing on his high platform in the center of the arena, struck a metallic staff against the metal and shouted a chant of "All hail King Taharqua!". The crowd followed, their only unity a droning call to hail a king who demanded their adoration, but did not desire their well being.

Soon, the crowd-noise subsided and the platform lowered slowly to the large metal space where many Terrans had lost their lives in gruesome ways. Nexu strode away, disappearing through a door in the wall of the arena that closed behind him abruptly. Soon another series of doors opened on the other side of the arena and three large rusting cages emerged, each floating on repulser sleds. Small clusters of Terrans were huddled inside each of them. The crowd above, upon seeing this spectacle, began to salivate in anticipation of the show that was about to begin.

A voice mumbled over the arena's broadcast comm system, and then it cleared its throat and began the introductions.

"We have traitors in our house," said the gravelly voice. "Traitors recycle to the void. Kiss the face of annihilation!"

Aura the bounty hunter, stripped of her gear, stood with them. She coughed as she breathed the stinking air, but frantically dug away at a spot on her wrist where she kept something buried just under her skin. She pressed at it as an elderly woman next to her stared on in horror.

"You better just give up, love," said the old woman. "We won't make it out of here alive."

Aura shot a glance at the old woman.

"Speak for yourself," she said, a slight grin forming across her lips. "I'm not out of this yet and neither are you."

"I don't have any illusions, dearie," replied the elder woman, gripping the bars of the cage with withered hands.

Aura pulled a small thread of metallic fiber from under her

skin and turned the little blood-caked thing over in her hand. Someone grabbed her wrist just then and she stared into the ragged face of a man whose dark hair hung over his steely eyes.

"I wouldn't do that if I were you," he said, his robotic hand squeezing her wrist a little too tightly. "Not only will you wreck the plan, but you'll get people I care about a lot more than you killed."

34

Commander Absalom Liberty, formerly Security Chief Absalom Liberty, formerly scourge of the tech-enhanced Phaedran shock troopers, scanned the bridge with enhanced eyes. He hunted weakness, waiting to pounce on any crew member not following orders to the letter or who moved with insufficient speed and accuracy.

"Any word on the drones," he growled. "My patience wears thin."

A gaunt warrant officer looked up from his console for a moment to respond.

"We have picked up a signal near the planet Exile, Commander," he said. "It appears that the Shibboleth world ship has emerged from FTL drive again."

Absalom's expression, unreadable to all around him, did not change.

"Spin up the FTL, navigator," he said coldly. "We will catch them unawares. At last we will be rid of their imperfection."

He pressed control studs at three panels on a raised holo-table before him and then moved toward the lift like a predatory animal. He spun to face his bridge crew before the doors closed, his iron gaze remaining in their minds even after he was alone in the lift.

"Deck thirty seven," he said, and the lift carried him there almost instantaneously.

As soon as the doors opened he sprinted down the corridor to Thorburn Plath's quarters. He thought about his goal, his desire to be absorbed into the consciousness of the AI. It would finally end the ages of struggle that his subordinates saw as a weakness. The AI and his conduits had denied him the one thing he wished to do, choosing instead to use his tech-born abilities as a living weapon of war.

Absalom Liberty desperately desired his own death, but the Conduit would not let him ascend.

He hesitated before the Conduit's quarters, the fingers of one hand flexing, and before he could press the call button the withered voice of the Conduit echoed from the comm panel near the door.

"Come in, Commander Liberty," he said. "I have been expecting you."

The door slid aside and Liberty strode in, the skeletal tattooing on his face a menacing mask in the near darkness of the room. His reddened eyes darted back and forth, scanning the room for the Conduit, until they rested on a shriveled form near a wide plasteel window which looked out on a blanket of stars. The ambient light in the room only revealed the silhouette of Thorburn Plath, but the various muted blinking lights on his eye-scopes gave him away.

"You have news for me, I suppose," said Plath.

Absalom dropped to one knee on the spartan floor, his fist pounding his chest once in salute.

"We have located the Shibboleth world ship, my lord. We are moving to intercept it as we speak. I shall shred their hull with our phase cannons and then we shall board what is left to insure their deaths. The Most High Computat will be pleased."

Absalom could see the eye-scopes of the elder Plath turn and focus in on him in the dark. He absently wondered how quickly he could snatch them out of the old man's head.

"You think of killing me," said Plath, his voice a wheeze. "Perhaps you would succeed, but it would not allow you to be released from your service to us, to ascend to higher consciousness. Without the capture of the three we will set back the Computat's plans decades, decades we will both live in this state."

Absalom bowed his head.

"Of course, Conduit," he whispered, knowing his every thought was being scrutinized. "Forgive me. I am conditioned for war. I am at your service."

A slight laugh escaped the withered lips, a shrill coughing echo fading away at the end.

"Absolutely," said the Conduit. "The Most High Computat will indeed grant your desire when you have eradicated the anomaly. But he desires to possess the three he has lost. The Shibboleth will fail in their effort to rescue the third, and in so doing they will be delivered into our hands."

"The third is on Exile?"

"Yes," said Conduit Plath, rising to his feet, the servos in his augmented legs straining. "We have known this for some time, and have made arrangements for her to be brought to us. The Shibboleth are walking into a trap we have devised for them. Our arrival over Exile and the destruction of their ailing world ship will be but the final step in the operation."

With a wave of the Conduit's narrow fingers Absalom was commanded to rise, and he obeyed.

"But Commander Ivory," said Absalom. "Her failure was part of the Most High Computat's plan as well?"

"Of course," chuckled the Conduit. "She was but the face

of welcome to lull the two children into a sense of belonging. They are the genetic key to the final ascension. Probability dictates that we should see benefit from this when we bring the three of them together again at the Citadel on Phaedra Prime. It will take some work, and some time, but we will succeed. The Most High Computat protects us and has worked out all possible outcomes. He is simply guiding us to that inevitable conclusion."

"And what is that?"

"What we all desire, of course. The final rest of all Terrans. The final step in our evolution. Pure augmentation. Transcendence."

35

"What do you mean I'll get your friends killed?" shouted Aura over the cacophonous noise of the arena. "And who are you anyway?"

Guillermo raised both hands in defense, preparing for a blow from her.

"We've got it all planned out...well...sort of," he said hastily. "But I'm pretty sure it will work. You just need to remain calm while we move a few pieces into place. My friends are working to get your daughter to safety first."

"My daughter?!"

Their heated conversation was interrupted by the sound of another blast from a metallic horn, a klaxon of such epic noise that everyone in the cage raised their hands to cover their ears. Guillermo peered through the bars to witness a large door dropping open onto the metal floor of the arena from the opposite wall. A creature emerged, something like an ancient rhino with a massive sea urchin for a head. Guillermo guessed that the spiny barb was its head because it moved in the direction it was facing, but he could not see eyes or a mouth.

It lumbered forward, and then another door dropped open

and the glare from something reflective caused him to cover his eyes. Something slithered out into the baking sun and scraped the metal floor of the arena with massive claws, rushing toward the spiny beast with undulating metallic scales reflecting the light like an ancient disco ball. It immediately pounced on the spiky creature and raked its claws into the victim's leathery hide.

Aura gripped the lattice work of the metal cage with her fingers, taking a deep breath.

"Shytaar!" she screamed.

Guillermo appeared next to her as the two beasts wrestled and clawed at one another, the rhino beast swinging around to stab its spines at the near impenetrable scales of Shytaar.

"That thing a friend of yours?"

She turned, her eyes filled with rage.

"Yes!" she shouted. "I raised him from a pup."

Guillermo peered through the bars.

"It appears he's doing pretty well for himself."

They looked on as the two creatures scuffled, Shytaar's talons scraping at the metal floor while the other beast's club-shaped feet stomped and pounded. It wasn't long before the rhino-beast fell to the floor and Shytaar was biting into its flesh to gobble a few scraps of meat from the dead creature. The crowd booed, the fight too quick for their taste.

"Shytaar!" Aura screamed again, then noticed a collar around Shytaar's neck. It held a black box with a blinking red light that winked on and off. Someone had also tied his wings to his back with heavy metallic bands.

She stepped back from the bars and turned toward Guillermo.

"They have a control box on him," she said. "I don't think he will help us."

"Ya think?" Guillermo scoffed. "Nothing ever seems to work out for me anyway...at least at first. If you hang out with me for long enough you find that out. I just figure out a way to skip past the worst of it."

She shot back a puzzled grin as a loud clang interrupted their conversation and another door dropped open across from them. Shytaar turned and crouched low to the arena floor, his long tail whipping back and forth and his heavy jaws opening wide in a defensive posture. Deep in the darkness of the newly revealed doorway a deep blue form slithered and writhed. It suddenly screeched out a threatening familiar call and Guillermo shuddered as an Ontoccan whiptail shot out of the darkness and scrambled across the arena toward Shytaar.

"Oh chert," Guillermo muttered as the crowd roared in approval. "Your pet is dead. That's a big one."

Indeed it was, one of the biggest Guillermo had ever seen, but Aura only glanced at Guillermo briefly before gripping the bars tighter and screaming her pet's name. She hoped to get him to listen to her voice, to adhere to her training, but the collar prevented the beast from listening. The box's mind control was complete.

The creatures struck at each other with lethal claws, the whiptail actually managing to pierce Shytaar's metallic hide with its scorpion-like tail. Guillermo wondered if the poison would effect this nanotechnological beast like it had done to him and to many other Ontoccans, but Shytaar fought on as if nothing was different. The two of them writhed around the center of the arena as one of the spectators came too close to the railing and was shoved over the edge, falling to the arena floor. He tried to run, but was trampled by the two scuffling beasts as they rolled toward the wall.

"Our only hope is if the other beast disables Shytaar's collar!" Aura yelled over the noise of the roaring crowd. "What did you have planned?"

"Not this," Guillermo said with a nervous chuckle. "I just

hope that the others figured out what to do next. If they did we should be hearing something about..."

He waited, his hands tensing, one eye closing.

Nothing.

And then there was an explosion far above them followed by raining bits of metal that dropped to the rusted, pock-marked floor, bouncing and clanging.

"Yep," he said. "There went the first repulser platform."

"My child is on one of those!" she screamed, and she shoved him down. Now she was towering over him, her nostrils flaring, eyes wide. "You said you'd rescue my baby! She has been brainwashed and is being used as a human shield!"

He raised his metallic wrist to his mouth.

"Mitsuki," he said flatly. "Did you get all that?"

Silence.

He looked at her, shrugged, and she raised her fist.

"Yes," came the tinny voice of Mitsuki, interrupting Aura's action. "We just took out the main guard platform. Adanez has identified the child and we are adjusting the plan. Dervish will extract her."

"Copy that," he said.

He stood to his feet, brushed himself off nonchalantly, and placed a hand on Aura's shoulder.

"We are doing our best," he said. "Just give us a chance."

Suddenly they were knocked to their feet as the two creatures, locked in a death roll, slammed into the Terran's cage. The Terrans within scrambled away, pressing toward the back of the cage as the two creatures traded slaps with clawed feet. Their razor maws gnashed and tore, shredding flesh and biting through metallic scales.

"We have to get that collar off of Shytaar!" Aura screamed.

They could suddenly hear plasma rifle blasts from far above, but the roof of the cage prevented them from seeing anything else. The two beasts continued to struggle, but they moved away from the cage, circling each other like two massive predatory lions, the whiptail nearly twice the size of Shytaar, but seemingly worse for wear. Gouts of greenish blood oozed from wounds on its side and neck. Then Shytaar slithered forward, darted under the gnashing jaws of the whiptail to latch onto the blue beast's waddled throat. Shytaar's teeth clamped down like a jagged vice, chomping until biting firm, and the whiptail gurgled out a low rattling hiss, clawing at its attacker with its heavy fore claws without much purchase.

The fight was nearly over, and the cages would soon be opened.

Guillermo thought that they all might make a tasty rewarding treat for Shytaar.

"Guillermo," came the tinny voice of Mitsuki over the comm. "We have the child, but we are pinned down. Do you think you can improvise?"

"I'm on it," he said, and he balled up his fist and pounded at the cage.

He pounded again and again, the rusting metal weakening with every blow, and then he began to glow a bright orange as his personal shielding kicked in.

He looked over his shoulder at Aura and the rest of them.

"You all ready to get out of here?"

One person at the back muttered something about the obvious and Guillermo simply shrugged and moved toward the lattice work of bars. He let out a roar and the shield bubbled out around him, devouring the metal, turning it to vapor, the air suddenly smelling of ozone.

"I'll release the rest," he said, his eyes ablaze. "You get your pet and get out of here. Not sure how long I can keep this up."

He ran out of the cage and took an abrupt left as he raced

toward the other two cages, a trail of crackling orange energy
trailing behind him. Aura emerged from the smoking hole
Guillermo had left in the cage and watched as her pet
finished off the whiptail with a twist of his head and then
dropped it to the deck to then turn and face her.

Hunger was in his glistening eyes.

Shytaar crouched low to the ground, the creature lumbered
toward her, its razor-filled mouth opening and slamming
shut, the screech of its metallic claws scraping the metal floor
of the arena. She came at him at a full sprint, readying herself
for what came next. She was determined to save Shytaar, her
only hope to remove the collar from his neck, damage that
device somehow.

Shytaar shot toward her, now at a gallop, his belly low to
the ground. She poured on the energy, watching for her
opportunity, trying desperately to suppress the idea that she
may not survive this. She reached out toward him as he came
closer. The skin on her neck tingled with fear. Her hand just
touched Shytaar's nose as he opened his maw. She vaulted
over him, landing astraddle his neck, her foot coming down
on the control box in an attempt to break it.

But it was solid.

She held on to the collar, grabbing tight as Shytaar rolled
over. She dodged the crushing blow of his right front talon
only to catch her foot between the band and one of his wings.
She felt her leg twist painfully, but she held on as Shytaar
righted himself and began to run toward a fleeing group of
Terrans. Suddenly jagged strips of metal and random small
parts from countless crashed starships rained down upon
them from the stadium seating above, thrown by ravenous
spectators. She ignored it, ignored the pain in her leg, and
began to strike at the control box with her fist, trying to
ignore the pain. Tears were welling up in her eyes as she saw
a blur of orange energy. Something struck Shytaar so hard

that he let out a strange whimper and fell to the hard arena floor.

It didn't knock him out, though, and he shook his head and growled.

Shytaar stood and she hung on, her fumbling hand finding a strange lump on the side of the control box. She pulled at it just as Shytaar knocked Guillermo across the arena with his powerful tail. Out of the corner of her eye she saw the reavers crawling down into the arena like a horde of metal-augmented arachnids, their shrieks causing a fear in her she had to quell. She pulled, fingers slipping, then she reached back around and pulled until she heard something pop.

The collar fell to the hard floor just as Guillermo was rising to his feet.

She fell to the floor of the arena beside Shytaar and he calmly turned toward her and sniffed, standing still as she managed to climb onto his back with a little help from his forepaw.

The reavers began to slice their way through the crowd of huddling Terrans, their screams filling the arena with horrific sound. Each reaver was a scrambled mess of sharpened metal legs and humanoid torsos, their heads a fright-mask of flesh and metal, their arms fitted with various cutting implements.

"Let's get them, Shytaar," said Aura.

And Guillermo and Aura waded into the reavers.

36

"Cut his wings loose!" Aura screamed as Shytaar bit down on the head and shoulders of an attacking reaver.

"With what?" shouted Guillermo, his glowing fists vaporizing two of them in a flash of orange light.

A flood of gnashing reavers came at them in a wave as tried to stand their ground. The scissoring metal sounds of knife-blade arms surrounded them even though Guillermo's shield expanded out to create a protective bubble. Shytaar struck at them with every appendage, his helpless wings strapped to his back with thick-fibered ropes.

"Climb on!" Aura shouted, and Guillermo complied, scrambling aboard the back of the chrome-plated beast as his shield contracted.

With a non-verbal command, Shytaar scrambled forward, leaping into the air. His long claws sliced into the metal walls as he broke through the jagged metal spikes and climbed higher and higher. Aura and Guillermo gripped tightly at the heavy ropes tying down Shytaar's wings as the creature managed to struggle to the first set of stands. Dozens of the more privileged citizens of Sanctum Mesa shrank fled in fear as Shytaar mounted the stands. Some did not escape, however, as Shytaar mowed through them, his tail knocking one of them into the waiting razor-arms of the reavers. The reavers pursued, like Terran cockroaches augmented with horrific buzz-saw and razor bladed implements scaling the walls of the arena and pouring over into the stands. Guillermo looked back at the horde of reavers approaching and felt his shield begin to fade.

"We'd better find a way out of here," he said. "I'm beginning to run out of energy I think. Never really happened before. Haven't used this ability at this strength before."

"Was this part of the plan?" she retorted.

He managed a thin laugh.

"Uh, yeah…I guess. I didn't think it could last forever."

Shytaar began to get his footing as he found an exit through a low tunnel. He slithered through and came to a halt as five of King Taharqua's personal soldiers in scrapped together armor appeared, their plasma rifles blasting at Shytaar's face. He shook it off, gnashed at them, and then barreled through them, knocking them over or stomping them under his heavy clawed feet.

On the other side Guillermo spoke into his wrist again, his voice cracking a bit when he looked behind him and saw the reavers approaching like a clustered mass of razor-sharp metal.

"Mitsuki, did you get that ship going?"

Silence, at least on the comm.

"Mitsuki!" he shouted.

Still nothing.

Shytaar galloped on, knocking over tables and booths as he raced through the giant bazaar where the Terrans of Sanctum Mesa traded. Screams echoed as he plowed along, citizens scrambling out of the way, some of them not quite making it before Shytaar ran them down.

"We have to get his wings free!" Aura shouted, pulling at the bands.

Guillermo felt the heavy cables with his free hand. He didn't think they would budge without a plasma torch or another heavy duty cutting implement. He decided to try calling Mitsuki one more time.

"Mitsuki!" he screamed. "Do you read me?"

A shadow fell over them, blotting out the oppressive sunlight, and two reavers leaped onto Shytaar's back and began slicing at Guillermo. He kicked one of them to the ground where the fiend tumbled and bounced, hissing out curses. The other one wrapped a jagged hand around Guillermo's arm and with needle-like metal teeth bit down on Guillermo's shoulder. Guillermo shouted and then gripped the reaver by his durasteel-plated skull. In a fit of rage and pain he crushed it like an egg.

The reaver fell away, his body sliding off Shytaar's rump like a bag of spare parts.

The shadow became darker, and above them a rush of wind blasted down, scattering debris around them as they rushed forward.

"Somebody call for a ride?" crackled the voice of Mitsuki over the comm. "Almost didn't make it. Still might not."

Suddenly the transport ship dropped down in front of them, a ramp descended, and Aura guided Shytaar right into the hold. The ramp raised as quick as it had descended. Immediately there was the sound of several clawed hands augmented by long blades scraping and raking at the hull outside, and Guillermo knew that the reavers had caught up to them.

He didn't have time for that, though.

"Whose piloting this rig?" he asked.

"Dervish," Mitsuki said appearing from behind Shytaar who shook his head side to side, his metallic scales sounding a strange jingle.

The three of them left Shytaar in the hold to rush to the cockpit where Dervish and Adanez were busy plotting a course to orbit. Aura fell behind when they entered the common area, her gasp barely audible as she spied her little girl lying in a stasis pod asleep, her little face grimy from over a month of neglect. Aura pressed her face against the plasteel bubble and took in a deep breath, letting it out in a moan that could be heard in the cockpit beyond. She sank to the deck, her chest heaving in and out rapidly. She managed to force herself to stand again, leaning against the canopy, splaying her fingers out against the plasteel and staring with tear filled eyes at her lost baby now found.

"We were able to get her out before the King detonated the vest," said Mitsuki appearing behind her. "She didn't want to come willingly, so Dervish had to knock her out."

"Dervish," Aura muttered. "Who is this Dervish?"

"A bug from the Five Rims worlds," Mitsuki said. "She's pretty good in a tight spot. Even better since the augmentation. You should have seen how brave..."

"There is no need," said Aura. "I am reunited with Eve. That's all that matters."

In the cockpit, Guillermo was looking out the front plasteel canopy. The yellow skies of Exile were fading to black, and soon he could see the stars twinkling in the vacuum of space. The ancient world ship, a massive, mushroom shaped rotating hunk of rusting durasteel, floated just in orbit. A trail of ionized plasma leaked from her hull just at the bottom of the stem. It would have been magical if Adanez didn't sound the alarm klaxon, sending them all into high alert.

Sitting in space just a few kilometers from the world-ship was the massive triangular shape of the Phaedran Dreadnaught *Victorum*. It lit up the darkness of space as it suddenly began carving a hole in the world ship with its super plasma gun.

37

"We have to dock with them immediately," said Adanez, her voice strangely calm. "They can't take much of that for long. Don't know if they'll wait this time."

"They have to wait!" Guillermo shouted. "We're the chosen ones or whatever."

All of the others ignored him and only stared out the front cockpit window at the horror that was the Phaedran mega-beam. It formed a bright blue line that penetrated the world ship's feeble shields and cut chunks of metal from the hull. The world ship fired back with its own out-dated lasers, but they performed more like focused beams meant to illuminate the dark than do any damage. The Phaedran dreadnaught simply shrugged off the world ship's attacks with ease, barely registering on the concave energy field outside its hull.

"Here they come," Mitsuki said as a cloud of Phaedran fighters swarmed out of the underside of the dreadnaught. "Somebody get on the guns!"

"Dervish, stay on the helm," Adanez ordered. "The rest of you to the guns. But I'll need your hands in the engine room again, Mitsuki."

Guillermo ran by Aura and gave her the signal, and they

both darted away to find the guns. Dervish plotted a new course as Adanez and Mitsuki raced to the engine room. Mitsuki, arriving in the engine room, began to make adjustments like a pro. She could hear the thump of the transport's guns as Guillermo and Aura went to work, but soon the energy needs of those weapons paired with the power drain of the engines and shields began to cause some of the conduits to glow faintly orange.

"How far are we?" shouted Mitsuki. "Can't we just teleport like last time? Form a wormhole!"

"No," Adanez barked. "Not enough power in this crate."

Dervish, her gaze scanning the control panel, her fingers making subtle adjustments, clicked her mandibles together in a sign of frustration as a crippled Phaedran fighter spun out of control and raced toward the cockpit window. She managed to drop the throttle enough to avoid it, but her scanners were also picking up the distortion of space-time around the Shibboleth world ship.

They were activating their FTL drive.

"Aura," shouted Dervish, frantically working the controls. "You need to drop the gun and get up here. I need assistance."

Aura appeared suddenly in the door, no readable expression, only nodding and taking the co-pilot seat as they both began the calculations for navigating the swarm of fighters.

"Mitsuki!" Adanez screamed. "Baby that engine. They'll need all the power they can get to slip us through that quantum field. One wrong move and we're vaporized!"

"Yes ma'am!" said Mitsuki, her hands shakily spraying a cooling foam on a line of red-hot conduits.

Adanez appeared at Mitsuki's side, an electro-wrench in hand. Mitsuki watched as Adanez pulled cables from one conduit and plugged them into another, her cold eyes set in stone even though huge electrical arcs fired millimeters from her skin. Soon she was shouting orders at Mitsuki and she did her best to follow them.

Back in the cockpit, the on-board lights suddenly dimmed and Aura and Dervish were pressed into their seats, the engines getting a boost from somewhere, and the ship moved rapidly toward a waiting hangar bay on the underside of the world ship. Aura aimed the ship toward it, doing her best to keep the aging maneuvering thrusters in check, but then she felt icy fingers grip her around the neck as an automata appeared from a nearby wormhole.

"We have a breach!" choked Aura, her hand fumbling for something to swing at the intruder.

Dervish held fast to the console as Aura struggled from her seat and pinned the automata to the wall with her back. She wrenched the metallic fingers from her neck and threw it through the door and to the deck plating where it scrambled and clawed along the wall until it righted itself and leaped on her again. Aura was suddenly locked in a wrestling match with this metallic being who had the advantage of being able to bend its joints in unnatural directions.

Out of the corner of her eye Aura noticed Dervish was not in her seat because two more automata had appeared near her as well.

Soon her automata had coiled itself around her like a thick metal cable. She felt the wind leave her lungs, but she grit her teeth, reached out, and pulled a power relay from the wall and jammed it into the automata's mouth, the flesh of her hand burning with the crackle of plasma. Sparks danced and fell along the deck plating as the automata writhed, and the current arced along the attacker's body until it connected again with Aura's skin. She ignored the pain and continued until the automata fell silent. It was then that she heard more of them emerging from wormholes nearby, and she leaped to her feet to repel them.

But the ship was listing to the side, the docking bay slowly passing out of sight through the cockpit view screen.

Back in the engineering bay several automata were emerging from wormholes and Mitsuki was wrestling with two of them. She dared not fire a weapon in the engine room, but soon Adanez joined in, kicking and punching at the metallic skeletons as they came skulking near her. The two women battled fiercely, Mitsuki using her small stature to her advantage and Adanez her brute strength. They soon stood back to back, the automata approaching from all sides. Adanez dove forward into a couple of them. She fought blindly, grabbing a newly formed bladed spear that grew from the hands of one of the attackers. She stabbed through two of them with it at once, then drew it out to impale another to the deck plating and kick a nearby automata who was trying to pull at the re-connected conduit.

"Get to the cockpit!" shouted Adanez. "I'll keep them busy here. Get to the cockpit and get us inside the hangar. We can fire off an EMP once we do."

"Last resort?" Mitsuki exclaimed.

Adanez only nodded, severing the head of one with her weapon. Mitsuki did not answer either, using her nimble skill to vault over two charging automata and land on the other side near the door. As she ran out the door she heard behind her: "Let me know when we are clear!"

Mitsuki didn't look back, rushing to the common area where several automata were fighting with Aura and Dervish. Guillermo's orange shield lit up walls as he fought bare-fisted. The guns were unmanned, the cockpit abandoned, and as more automata appeared on the deck she knew they were fighting for their immediate survival. Aura was struggling with two of the attackers and Mitsuki rushed past her to just outside the cockpit.

They were spiraling out of control, diving toward the distant planet Exile.

Striking another automata with an extended elbow, Mitsuki plowed her way into the cockpit to re-position the ship on a course toward the hangar bay of the world ship. It was now twice the distance than before.

She slapped the comm controls.

"Terran cargo ship to Shibboleth world ship," she shouted into the stale air. "We are on our way. Under heavy attack. Taking on boarders. Prepare for crash landing. Don't spin up FTL yet."

Static.

"Attention cargo ship," came a frantic female voice. "We can only wait for fifteen more seconds. FTL already spun up and hot."

"Chert," groaned Mitsuki.

Suddenly she heard a roar behind her, a primal shout that reverberated from the walls of the common area. Guillermo was plowing through automata like a sickle through wheat. Mitsuki turned again to look to the front and saw the hangar bay door looming in the darkness. The barely-functioning running lights of their cargo hauler washed the grimy hull with a faint glow. She slammed the throttle forward, flipping on all the afterburners.

She pressed the comm.

"Adanez," she said, another automata pulling at her arm. "We are lined up with the bay!"

The deck plating seemed to be suddenly pulled out from under them as the inertial dampers failed. The ship punched forward through the darkness of space but was suddenly rocked with a loud bang as the landing gear were sheered away by the lower lip of the hangar bay door. Mitsuki felt her stomach flip slightly as the FTL engaged, and as she turned to attack the grasping, clawing automata she saw

Dervish, Guillermo and Aura destroy the last of the invading mechanical drones.

"Adanez!" she shouted again, running to the engineering bay where several desiccated automata lay scattered about the rusty deck plating. As the other three joined her, she knelt to the floor, her eyes wide, and took in an audible breath.

Lying among the scattered remains of the automata was the lifeless body of brave Clover Adanez.

38

Commander Absalom Liberty stood among the crumpled bodies of the super laser tech crew, his thick and bloodied hands folded behind his back. A hole had been torn in the hull so that the planet Exile could just be seen hanging in space, the debris from the world ship and his own Phaedran dreadnaught mingling in zero gravity. An emergency forcefield protected him from the vacuum of the void, and as he watched the crews of nervous Phaedran engineers clearing away the rubble he managed a small half-smile as he surveyed the damage.

The clanking of automata stomping across the deck plating was the only prelude to the skulking figure of Conduit Thorburn Plath, his ocular enhancements whirring and focusing as he hobbled forward. Absalom did not turn to acknowledge him, choosing instead to stare out at Exile and think about what might befall him.

"You have failed me, Absalom," hissed the Conduit, his mouth dripping with a thick saliva. "Should I reclaim the gifts AI has given to you like those of your predecessor?"

Absalom's arm was a sudden blur as his hand shot out and lifted the Conduit from the floor by his neck. The automata around them struck at the Commander, but his personal shield prevented them from doing any damage, their arms burning away in a vapor of metallic mist.

"You forget your place, Conduit," growled Absalom, the wrinkled skin of the Conduit's neck sizzling and popping. "You forget that I am older than you, than the AI. That I am not under your control. That I have one goal: to see to the destruction of the Shibboleth. Your meddling, your desire to turn the bug into an ally has cost us dearly. I should have killed that bug when we found her on that ship with Guillermo and Mitsuki."

"This is insubordination!" Plath choked. "You will be…"

"I will be what?" Absalom grinned. "I was putting down Guajiin rebellions when you were still a low level technician. The only reason you are where you are is because you activated the AI again. I don't trust it, and I don't trust you. It is bureaucracy like yours that stands in the way of progress."

Absalom's vice-like hand opened and the Conduit fell to the floor. Two automata gingerly helped him to his feet, and he immediately clutched his throat with trembling hands, his breathing an augmented wheeze.

"You had better find them, Commander," he croaked. "If you do not, then no amount of veteran status will save you from the Most High Computat…may his mercy ever be flowing. Your only hope of ending your eternal servitude is to do His will, and I am the conduit for that will. I will forgive this insubordination because I need your leadership, but understand that I only tolerate you as long as you are needed."

Absalom chuckled as the Conduit was led away by the automata, the old man's step stumbling now and again so that an automata had to catch him and right him again. Absalom placed both hands behind his back again, turned, and saw the spindly frame of the bug queen emerge from the door after the Conduit exited. She turned to look at him, her dark compound eyes reflecting the orange glow of sparks that fell from repair crews working to restore the hull. Absalom stood as a statue, his dark eyes following her as she slinked forward, eventually placing one claw-like hand on his thick shoulder.

He sneered at her, but she clicked her damaged mandibles together and emitted a low hiss.

"I trust you have found all of the traitors on your ship," she mused, her mandibles clicking together to mimic Terran speech. "Too bad they were manning the super-laser."

Absalom folded his enormous arms over his chest and glared at her.

"I surmised they were aboard," he said. "At least now they are gone and we can be assured that my crew is loyal."

"Can you? My species are much easier to control. I have assured their obedience. Perhaps you could use this kind of power in your army."

Absalom glared at her, his rage rising.

"What do you want, bug? I don't have the time to offer favors or any alliance you had with the good doctor. I feel that your presence in our sector is an invasion. I do not share the alliances you have brokered with my superiors."

She slinked up to him, her face a few millimeters from his.

"You need us, Terran," she hissed. "You must co-exist with my subjects. You cannot afford a war with me. Besides. I still have sway over one in their company. Soon she will fill her role."

He pushed her aside and strode from the room, three armored Phaedran soldiers following him, and she looked on, her mind whirring with the plan she had discussed with Doctor Spurling before he met his demise at the hands of her former palace guard. If her physiology would have allowed her to grin she would have, as she ran her nimble finger along the C'Tuul'U'Hindra upon her brow, the ancient device that allowed her to communicate with and control her kind.

At her command, she saw in her mind's eye her armada of bug cruisers and dreadnaughts emerging from the ionic cloud as well as the inside of the Shibboleth world ship.

These Terrans cannot be trusted. It is time for them to face the reality that they are not the superior species. Now we will take what is ours, and I will have my revenge on Guillermo once and for all.

39

Adanez's lifeless body, covered in a blanket found in the common area of the transport, was carried delicately down the landing ramp by members of her engineering crew as a great crowd of Terrans looked on. Her children stood in a row, the two oldest with head bowed low, little Dana held by her nanny Ulah. Dana's little face was pressed into Ulah's shoulder, hiding her eyes from the spectacle. Death was a common fact of life among the Shibboleth, and even though this was true, the little ones could still barely grasp the concept.

Mitsuki held on to Guillermo's arm, her face wet with tears.

"I had to leave her for just a little while," she said. "I feel like its my fault."

Guillermo placed a hand gently on her arm.

"Nothing you could have done, Mitsuki," he said, his voice low and even. "She did what was necessary to keep the engines running. We are here because she wouldn't give up. We won't forget her sacrifice. I'll make sure of that."

Elder Priestess Iona Jung, her robes wrapped about her like a shroud, pulled her hood up to cover her grey hair. She held her wrinkled hands aloft, crooked fingers splayed out, and the crowd all turned to face her. Their faces were ashen, downcast eyes among them all, for they had lost an integral part of their family.

"Clover Adanez was a great leader of our people," Iona said, her voice wavering slightly. "She gave her life for the cause, for Eden, and so did many others. I have received word that many of our hidden cells have activated. They have given their lives to disrupt the machine that is the Phaedran Empire, so she is not alone. Clover's gift to us is that we are alive to fight another day, and now that we have the three children in our grasp we shall soon see the promised paradise for which we have earnestly prayed. No longer will we have to sacrifice our friends and family for the cause, for we shall by God's grace be free of oppression."

The crowd all bowed their heads in unison, each of them folding their hands, their lips murmuring prayers. The crew holding the body of Adanez lay her gently down and joined in the posture of the others. As Guillermo, Mitsuki and Aura took their place beside the body, Dervish fell behind, bracing herself against a bulkhead as if she were exhausted, her ovoid head lowering.

Guillermo's eyes flashed about the room. In this room full of palpable sadness he was only filled with rage. He could only stare at Adanez's children and feel completely helpless as they wept.

But he would not weep.

He grit his teeth, thinking about the injustice done to him on the bug planet, to his fellow Terrans, people he had taken for granted and had thought of as lower-class citizens before they were wiped out by a well-placed bomb. He had bought into the culture that his race was on its way out, washed up, on the end of their journey as a species. His mind was drawn to a faint memory of his long-deceased wife, a woman who kept him grounded until she was given a drug that immediately hooked her on a downward spiral to death. He thought about his own life, about how selfish he had been, about how this remnant of Terrans didn't deserve the curse brought on them by their Phaedran ancestors. Above all, he was just tired of losing the battle and losing good people like Adanez.

"When are we going to take these *v'oshtu's* out?" he blurted.

Guillermo felt a sharp pain in his side and turned to see Mitsuki's angry glare.

"Have some respect, Guillermo," Mitsuki hissed. "They just lost many of their friends and family...and so did we."

"We've all lost many of our loved ones," Guillermo said firmly, the crowd parting for him. "If we don't do more than just suicide missions then what makes the Terran race worth saving won't be worth a burned out plasma coil."

Dervish slumped against the wall, slid down to the floor and collapsed.

"We are not quite ready to mount our final attack on the AI just yet, Guillermo," said the Priestess. "There is much to discuss...much to prepare...before we send the three of you in to do what you were bred to do."

"Guillermo," Mitsuki said.

He turned to her, expecting to find that accusing frown, but instead found her kneeling over the quivering body of Dervish. The crowd began to murmur as Guillermo ran to Dervish, knelt beside her and took her claw-like hand.

"What's wrong with her?" he asked, but Dervish stirred momentarily. She raised her head shakily, her mandibles clicking and whirring in the mimicry of Terran speech.

"It is the queen," she chittered. "She is alive and she is bringing her armies here."

"Why?" Guillermo asked. "She's been working with the

Phaedrans all along, I suppose."

"She is planning the revenge of our people, revenge for centuries of slavery. Yet she has more grand designs than this. She plans to enslave all others who are not of our kind. She is still trying to control...me...but I am fighting..."

The elderly Priestess appeared at Guillermo's side, placing a hand on Dervish's quivering chest. With her other hand she produced a tiny whirring box that she placed just beneath Dervish's left eye. Dervish winced and her mandibles splayed out and quivered for a moment before a small transparent spider emerged from behind a compound eye. The old woman snatched it up and crushed it in her bony hand.

Dervish fell silent, her abdomen slowly rising and falling.

"It is the control device," the Princess explained. "The Queen was attempting to use your friend against us. She will need rest. We must be as determined as your friend, here. Her bravery is admirable."

She motioned to two soldiers.

"Take her to the infirmary," said the Priestess. "She will be better soon."

Guillermo and Mitsuki stood as Dervish was taken from the hangar bay and gingerly helped along by two strong soldiers. Aura looked on along with a host of other Terrans who began to gather around Guillermo and Mitsuki as if huddling for an ancient Earth game.

"Friends," said Priestess Jung to the onlookers. "Return to your stations. The engineering crew will take poor Adanez to her rest, and then we will continue on as we have always done. We will not be deterred until we see Eden. We will not let these sacrifices be in vain."

A unified voice was heard then, a simple "we will obey", echoing from the vaulted ceiling of the hangar bay.

When the Terrans began to disperse, the Priestess turned to

the three of them.

"And now we will discuss the plan to return us to our home."

40

They sat around a grey table built into the rusting floor plates, the low rumble of the engines barely perceptible, and everyone seemed to be fighting the same sense of dread brought on by the death of Adanez. Guillermo couldn't stop thinking about her children, especially the little one who could only bury her face in her nanny's shoulder. He scanned the room, his eyes falling on the strangers sitting around the table, his assumption being that they were somehow leaders of this Shibboleth insurgence. All of them seemed to be as old as the Priestess or older save one young woman who sat next to the Priestess, apparently an attendant or priestess of their order.

A yellow light flickered along the edges of the low ceiling where several panels had been removed long ago and various conduit splices hung freely, a constant reminder of the engineer's handiwork. Guillermo thought that Adanez must have patched and re-patched this ship many times, leaving her fingerprints behind on every device and system. Mitsuki sat with arms folded next to Guillermo and Aura stood at the door, her hands behind her back, her red hair falling about her shoulders.

Just then Dervish limped past her, walking slowly, and then sat next to Guillermo. She placed her clawed hands on the table and clicked two mandibles together.

"You heal fast," Guillermo said. "Whatever you're drinking, I want some."

She didn't respond, not seeing his lips move. He gently touched her arm and mouthed the words again.

"I am fine," Dervish croaked loudly. "But I have news for your—"

"The Empire must be eradicated," Aura interrupted coldly, her mouth a thin line. "The plan to leave this space and return to Eden is sound, but too many have died. We cannot leave this sector without destroying the hierarchy led by the AI. You sent me on a surveillance mission, Priestess, and the Phaedrans captured my daughter and sold her to that fat king on Exile. She'll never be the same. She's resting right now, but I would say that these Phaedrans are just the same as they always have been: completely depraved...anarchists. They are planning to dominate all known space, and if we don't take them out they will eventually reach Eden...if it exists. How do I assure the safety of my daughter's future...her children's future... if we uproot and leave?"

The old woman held a hand out toward Aura.

"All in good time," she said. "Once the AI is destroyed we believe its hold on our fellow Terrans will be broken. Without organization they will either destroy one another or find new leadership. We have to hope that they will return to their better natures. The Shibboleth movement began with only a few people centuries ago, helped the Five Rims planets free themselves from Phaedran rule, and ultimately helped them exile our fallen Terran brothers and sisters to this sector of the system. It is my hope that we can have a positive effect on the Phaedran Empire and lift the curse of violence and domination within our species."

Aura rolled her eyes.

"You are dreaming if you think the Phedrans will come around," she snarled. "In the guise of a bounty hunter I witnessed unbelievable cruelty among their ranks. They prize augmentation by the AI, believing that being augmented is what makes them closer to godhood. They worship that thing, calling it the Most High Computat. The AI has realized the common weakness in the Terran mind, that of blind faith in a believed truth. These Phaedrans follow the AI like it's a god. How are we to fight that?"

"We must have faith that God, the true God of the universe, can turn their wicked minds to the truth," countered the Priestess.

"This faith is the same as theirs," Aura retorted. "You believe in a God of Earth who is found in a book that can't be verified as truth. The only difference between us and them is that your faith is one of peace. We give in. We plant our cells throughout the Empire to sew seeds of our faith and disrupt when it serves our cause, but in the end we aren't much different from them."

The Priestess stood to her feet, one wrinkled hand pushing up from the table for support.

"I know you have sacrificed much for this cause, Aura, as many of us have. However, I believe we are finally coming to the end of our struggle, that the return of these other two children is indeed providence. They have been gathered to us at a time when our cause is at its weakest and most vulnerable. The FTL drive is soon to fail as we only have one or two more jumps until it ruptures. Our food and water supplies are nearing an end. The AI is closing in on us as we speak and it won't be long before they figure out that we are hiding in FTL limbo. I know you have suffered much, Aura, but you must understand that we are so close to ending this conflict once and for all. Please do not give up now. You,

Mitsuki and Guillermo are the key to defeating the AI, the Phaedran Empire, and to bringing us all to Eden safely and without future threat."

Aura, her face growing wan throughout the Priestess's heartfelt speech, moved quietly to the table and sat beside Mitsuki.

"Forgive me, Priestess," she muttered. "I shall comply for now. Please tell me you have a viable plan. My daughter's future is counting on it."

The Priestess sat, her attendant holding her hand for stability.

"The plan is in motion as we speak. Cells all over the Empire have been notified via our secret communication network, and they are willing to do what is necessary to help us succeed. We must first run more tests on you three before we are sure the plan will work. We are not entirely sure the code within your DNA will line up. If it does line up, then we know that the AI will be destroyed. There is still a small chance it will not. Now that we have all three of you together and you have fully matured we can see if what we did worked."

"Fully matured?" asked Mitsuki.

"Yes," said the Priestess. "The code needed to mature...to grow and replicate within your cells until it had been imprinted on all of your DNA."

Guillermo stood to his feet, the chair tipping over and falling behind him with a crash. Dervish moved to stand the chair back up, then placed a clawed hand on Guillermo's shoulder and buzzed something in his ear. Guillermo's eyes widened as he plopped back down in his chair.

"Holy Temple of Ch'hut," he said, turning to Dervish. "You sure?"

"Yes," she said. "I saw everything through the connection."

"Please explain, Guillermo," said the Priestess.

"Dervish here says the Queen is in this sector and she's playing the Phaedrans, working with them only to conquer them. She's bringing her armies through the ionic cloud."

There was a murmuring about the table, and one of the elders spoke up.

"Is this the Queen of the bug species?" he asked. "And what does it have to do with the —"

"Everything!" Mitsuki interrupted. "She's the leader of the bug home world. Real evil chu'hrak, unlike her mother whom she assassinated. She has already conquered the Five Rims, and if she brings her horde through the ionic cloud under the Phaedran's noses... If she does that..."

"All will be lost," said Dervish. "She has technology once used by our people to dominate the Five Rims when your kind were living in caves. Our people buried it, locked it away and chose to live a simpler life. She has awakened this technology and she uses some of it to control all of my kind. If she brings her hordes through the ionic cloud, she will outnumber the Phaedrans. She may possibly win."

For a moment the only sound that could be heard was the rumble of engines far below.

"Our only hope is to bring down the AI," said the Priestess, her face set like stone. "Its destruction is the key to bringing peace to the region, free the Terrans from its grip, and to forge a path to Eden. The Queen's war against Terrans is, I suppose, a remnant of the curse brought upon us for the indiscretions of our past. We will flee to Eden. The rest will pay for their iniquity."

"So we are going to resign some of our race to apocalypse in order to see to the safety of a few?" Guillermo said. "I have no love for the Phaedrans, but ultimately they are Terran like us. We need assurances. Clover Adanez's kids need assurances. If the Queen is working with the

Phaedrans, it's assured she's only doing it to garner false trust. With one hand she welcomes them, but with the other she motions her armies to attack. This is all bigger than just saving the Terran race. How can we assure ourselves that the Queen won't come looking us up on Earth, and that's if it exists? Also, if we are going to risk our necks infiltrating Phaedra Prime, then we need to know how this code of yours is going to work. Is there some way we can test it out small scale?"

"In the past we theorized that we could capture a drone," offered one of the other elders. "But then we realized that it would alert the AI to our location and we would run the risk of losing everything."

"I could work on a way to mask its outgoing signals," Aura offered. "I jury-rigged a lot of tech while posing as a bounty hunter. I've learned a lot about their newest tech and I think I could manage to fool those algorithms."

"All the drones that materialized inside the world-ship have been destroyed," Guillermo said. "We all made sure of that. Think you could use some of their spare parts to do the test?"

"Sure," she said. "It's worth a shot."

A few eyebrows raised on faces around the table.

"So, once I get one of those drones working," Aura asked. "How do we interface?"

The Priestess cleared her throat.

"It is not known," she said. "You three are unique. We assumed that we would place you in contact with the AI and the rest would...take it's course. The original plan was to use the FTL drive to emerge just inside the defense grid of Phaedra Prime. You were to pilot a shuttle down to the capital using the coordinates sent to us by our operatives and then you would just interface with the AI."

"Interface?" Mitsuki asked, her shoulders squaring. "You

keep using that word. What do you mean by 'interface'?"

"Yes," said the Priestess. "It is a certainty you would be captured and the AI would want to speak to you in person as is its protocol. Once inside the citadel, you would...well... you would interface. You would simply do what you were *designed* to do."

Guillermo folded his hands in front of him on the table and lowered his head.

"I don't know what you mean," he said, trying to keep calm. "And what you you mean 'designed?'"

"No, we...," she smiled uncomfortably. "We are not sure what you are to...we are sorry. We trust that God knows the solution...that you will do what you are designed to do."

Guillermo stood abruptly and Mitsuki only stared at the table.

"I'm very ready to go take on the AI," he said, his face turning red. "I usually do pretty well flying by the seat of my trousers, but I've been through enough scrapes to learn that what we are about to do requires a little thinking through. And you still haven't answered my question. What do you mean by 'designed'?"

One of the elders across the table raised his hands as if he were about to be struck with a rod.

"We are sorry!" he said, his voice strained, a strange little gurgle escaping his throat. "When we rescued you from the facility on Phaedra Prime we did not know your purpose... why you were encased in the artificial wombs we found you in. We barely made it out of there alive, son. Many of our number sacrificed their lives to rescue you. You were the only Terran life-forms in that place without mechanical augmentation, and when we studied you we found the strange biomechanical properties of your DNA which allowed us to do what God had told us to do...encode your cells with His word."

The Shibboleth Code

41

"This," Guillermo exclaimed, pointing a finger at each of the elders as if counting them. "Is a collection of crulling senility and nonsense."

"No," interrupted the Priestess looking around at her fellow elders, eyes wide. "They must know! You are not Terran... at least not Terran in a sense that you are born from Terrans. You were created by the AI, automata created at the atomic level as *facsimiles* of Terrans. You were destined for something else...something for which we could only speculate. But we have, by the grace of God, given you a new purpose...encoded you with what *will*...we *hope*...bring down the AI."

One of the others spoke, his voice strained and withered by age.

"It is, we suppose, the reason the doctors who gave you your mechanical arm could not clone a replacement arm from your DNA. Your DNA is artificial, like that of the automata we have encountered here, but much more highly advanced. It is not biological, and yet it is. The three of you appear biological, but you are not. The three of you are fabrications. It is of a technology that seems as magic to our current levels, far beyond anything we could ever have created. It is no wonder the Phaedrans worship the AI as a god."

Aura, Mitsuki and Guillermo sat in silence. Aura stood to her feet, approached the doorway with arms folded, and rested her forehead against the door frame.

"We did not want to tell you this," said the Priestess. "It was our plan to return you to the AI with the code intact and our prayer was that it would interfere with the AI's code. Disrupt it. We speculate that the plan that the AI had for you and the children in that facility was to replace the Terran race, to conquer completely and perhaps spread out throughout the galaxy as it once planned early in our history. We shut it down then, and we must do the same this time, but it has grown beyond our technical knowledge."

"What do you mean you shut it down before?" Guillermo asked, his voice sounding small and soft.

"The days before the exodus to the Five Rims were desperate," said one of the other elders, stroking his grey beard. "As the story was handed down to me, the Terran race ran out of vital supplies, had completely used up the resources in their home solar system, and so AI was created to solve these problems, to save lives, and to invent an FTL drive to ferry our people to a distant star...the Five Rims. At first it made things better, taking over many of the already automated functions of production and mining. It made our ancestor's lives highly efficient. However, in time it believed, it *realized*, that the Terran race was merely a tool to a greater aim: complete conquest of all life in the universe. Several brave Terrans fought a war against it, a war which nearly wiped out our species. In the end we shut it down, but it had destroyed any hope of creating an FTL drive. Our people built the great world ships and traveled here, a journey made much longer without the ability to fold space."

The Priestess stood to her feet, and the rest in the room

could only look on her with tired eyes.

"The three of you were intended, were created, for an evil purpose. But we redeemed you from the AI, and now we will send you in again to bring about its final destruction. At least, that is our hope. We do not know if you will survive it, but we hold out hope that you will. We believe that you are our salvation. This is why our people have sacrificed themselves, have exposed their rebel cells when they did, because we all know that the success of your return to the AI is what we hope will be an end to our suffering."

Guillermo leaned forward and placed both hands on the table, looking left and right at the faces of those who had been with him throughout his journey that began on the bug home world.

"Let Aura here try to test out this interface you talk about," he said. "If it works, then we'll gladly go do what we can to take down the AI. I don't know what that will look like. I don't even know if what you just told me is the truth. All I know is that Aura gave up her life to get us here, and I will do anything I can to pay her back for that. I've lived a pretty selfish life, and if that means I have to redeem myself by doing a suicide mission, then that's what it means."

He looked around him, seeing the stern faces of Aura, Mitsuki and Dervish. Dervish he couldn't read, but that didn't phase him. He knew what she thought.

"I got these people with me," he said finally. "And I know that I have a better chance coming back alive with them than without them."

Dervish stood then, her head nodding, her clawed hands folded in front of her.

"I believe I can stop the Queen," she chittered, and Guillermo chuckled softly. "I must infiltrate the Phaedran ship where she is residing and kill her myself. Only then will I be able to free my people from her control. It will solve the issue regarding her desired domination of this system."

They all turned to stare at Dervish, and she only clicked her mandibles together nervously. Guillermo suddenly realized he couldn't read her thoughts after all.

"Priestess," offered the bearded elder. "If Dervish succeeds, it will be the final piece to a viable plan. What resources could we spare to help her? Providence has indeed smiled on this meeting."

"Now hold on right there, old fellah," Guillermo interrupted. "She's not doing this! I'll need her down on that Phaedran home world."

"Guillermo," Dervish said. "Please do not interfere. Your destiny lies with the AI. The path is very clear."

Guillermo shoved her shoulder with one firm hand.

"No way, old girl," he said. "You've been with me through a lot, and I really need you on this one."

Dervish stood her ground.

"Guillermo," she said, both of her clawed hands resting on his shoulders in some attempt at affection. "Please allow me this task. I must free my people. The Queen has corrupted the very nature of my species, a species that long ago gave up on aggression and conquest. She has set us back centuries with her warmongering. My people need to be free, and I know that I have the ability to end her tyranny. She controls my people against their will, uses a device that should have been destroyed ages ago to do it. If you truly care for me, you will let me do this."

Guillermo's steely-eyed gaze fell then, his mouth becoming a thin line.

"Ok girl. But you have to come with us. You have to promise you'll come with us."

"I cannot."

Guillermo could only stare at her as she tried clumsily to embrace him, held him close to her, and he slowly raised his arms to do the same. Moments later, the elders had cleared out of the room leaving Dervish and her three Terran allies alone.

"You could have told us this earlier," said Guillermo. "Why didn't you tell us this earlier?"

"I have been considering my options," Dervish said. "I had to determine the most logical and thereby feasible choice to the problem of the Queen. The Shibboleth plan is very logical, but it lacked one final piece. I must save my people, for you are about to do the same for yours."

Guillermo let out a long sigh.

"And you think going it alone to kill the Queen will be the most logical choice?"

"Yes."

"Well," Guillermo said. "We can't let you go it alone. We'll just have to figure out how to get you some help."

42

In a dim room deep within the upper levels of the *Victorum*, a lone figure sat hunched over a hologram. The holographic image, displayed in chromakey green, was of the outside of a battered hull. As the holographic image moved, the emerald light danced across the withered and pock-marked face of Conduit Thorburn Plath. His bony fingers danced over the controls, causing the image to shift and fluctuate. Soon a round porthole emerged on the landscape of green. He moved his palsied hand over the control stud carefully, revealing humanoid figures sitting around a round holographic table.

"Track thirty degrees down," croaked Plath. "Then zoom in on sector three-two-seven."

There was a whirr like the sound of several tiny electric motors and soon he could make out the familiar faces of three Terrans and a Bug. Plath's eyes, long ago replaced with highly sensitive optic scanners took in the many shapes and details revealed by the hologram. They were much more efficient than the naked eye, the thick goggles like two camera lenses taking every nuance and translating it directly to a mechanically enhanced brain.

He fiddled with the controls again, sending his distant camera to another porthole where he looked in on a room containing the phrenetic activity of humanoid forms rushing around from console to console. Even though he couldn't pick up sound he could make out the read-outs on one of the myriad devices. It was a navigation array, and as he zoomed in with his remote camera he could make out a series of numbers that plotted a four-vector location. With a flick of a gnarled finger, he saved the image and then ordered the single automata clinging to the hull of the world ship to self-destruct.

He cleared his throat.

"Conduit Plath to Commander Liberty," he said, his voice thin and airy, still healing after his brush with the techno-warrior.

The Commander appeared in the form of a chromakey green hologram before him, his skull tattoo superimposed on his rugged face.

"Yes, Conduit," he droned. "I live... to serve."

"I am sending the coordinates of the world ship now. I believe it is frozen in FTL drive and we should, with proper coaxing of the engines, be able to intercept the rebels with ease."

"Yes, Conduit. But it is too risky to take the *Victorum* to FTL limbo. I have prepared a juggernaut shuttle and have loaded it with our more advanced automata. I will make the necessary adjustments to the navigation computers myself. They will not escape us this time."

On the bridge, Absalom Liberty managed a vile grin before switching off the holographic emitter and rushing out of the bridge with three engineers hot on his heels. His mind whirled with the possibilities, the desire to finally bring his long life of suffering to an end, to be absorbed completely into the AI, to finally ascend. His reward would be exquisite.

"Commander," offered one of the engineers. "If I may, I believe there is a slight risk that we might be locked in FTL limbo. Have you considered the possibility that…"

"Do what you must," growled Absalom. "I will quash this Shibboleth threat myself. It will no longer threaten the Most High Computat and we will all be rewarded for our success."

"Yes, Commander. I live to serve."

43

The torso of an automata lay cracked open on an examination table as Aura plugged various cables and optic wires into a few ports she had discovered inside. It looked like a chrome rib cage, but with some study she had discovered that its "brain" was actually a slave-circuit that was operated remotely.

"Did you lock down the room?" she asked Mitsuki.

"Yes," Mitsuki said, fiddling with a wrist holo. "As good as we can. We could only do better if we set off an electromagnetic pulse. Of course we don't know if that will work or not on this tech."

Two engineers looked on, both of them very young. Aura spent most of her time explaining procedures to them and then explaining the same task again.

"I've seen this level of tech before," Aura explained as she used a micro-welder to attach a cable. "Helped me tame Shytaar."

Mitsuki waved her hand through a few algorithms.

"Oh," she said. "Where is your big metal friend?"

"Down in the hold," she replied. "He made a nest down there out of old junk. I really miss the big guy already. I sent

Guillermo down there to feed him."

Aura attached one more line, then stepped back from the table.

"You and Guillermo are pretty close, I gather."

Mitsuki looked up from her work for a second to flash a gaze at Aura.

"Yeah," she said. "We've been through a lot together."

"You think the two of you will be able to have a life together," asked Aura. "After the mission, I mean?"

"I don't know," Mitsuki said, and with only the sound of their frantic hands working with microfibers and transmitter arrays she began to let that last statement sink in. She thought about Guillermo and what they had shared, even if it seemed to be just shared smiles and a passionate kiss now and again, but she didn't know if she could live without him. The mission was, by all accounts, one from which they might not return.

Aura interrupted Mitsuki's thought process by clearing her throat after adjusting a few more leads.

"Ok," she said. "Here goes nothing."

"Don't say that," said Mitsuki, and Aura only glanced up before looking back down at her patient.

"We have to isolate the carrier signal and make sure that it doesn't broadcast. I've pretty much disabled it physically, burned the chert out of it with a micro-welder, but just to make sure we've dampened the room. Is Guillermo coming back up here to help us out in case...?"

A thud was heard and he entered the room.

"Don't ever ask me to do that again," Guillermo said, appearing at the door. "That thing is nightmare fuel."

Aura and Mitsuki shared a knowing smile as Guillermo moved over to stand just behind Mitsuki. She felt his hand rest on the small of her back which gave her a strange electrical charge. She glanced back over her shoulder at him and he smiled.

"Alright," Aura said with a smirk. "All we have to do is place our hands on this rib-cage here and hopefully we will somehow interface with this automata. At least that's what I think will happen."

"Do we do it all at once or one at a time?" asked Guillermo.

Aura looked at Guillermo, her eyes squinting in thought.

"We can try one at a time I suppose. Guillermo, you want to —-"

Guillermo grabbed the chromed rib cage with his mechanical hand.

The three of them stared at each other for a moment, and then Guillermo let out a sharp scream that echoed in the small room. Mitsuki and Aura began to move quickly, Mitsuki waving her hand over the wrist holo frantically, Aura reaching for her tool box.

And then Guillermo was laughing.

"Guillermo!" Mitsuki exclaimed, elbowing him in the side. "How can you possibly make a joke out of this? People's lives are at stake."

"Just wanted to lighten the moo—"

Suddenly Guillermo froze. His eyes widened, and he felt as if he were leaving his body. He stared at the automata on the table, his face an open-mouthed expression of amazement.

"Guys," he said softly, almost inaudible. "You have to try this. I'm somehow all over the ship. I can see Shytaar down in the hold eating that protein block. Ugh. I can also see the — woah. Whoops. The Priestess is indisposed."

He pulled his hand free and backed away, shook his head and blinked his eyes as if trying to clear them.

"Um. I'm still jacked in," he said. "Oh and there's an automata on the hull of this ship right now broadcasting our coordinates within FTL limbo. I'll just follow that signal to see where it's goin—"

Guillermo took in a deep, sudden breath of air and his face contorted with pain.

"Guillermo!" Mitsuki screamed as she waved her hand over the wrist holo frantically.

Red lights flashed as Guillermo fell to the floor and began to writhe, moaning loudly, his eyes rolling up to the top of his head. Mitsuki started for him, but backed away from the table in shock. The automata torso moved once, then fresh metallic skeletal arms began to sprout from its damaged shoulders.

"Cut the power!" Aura screamed. One of the engineers tried to do as she said, but Aura had to run over and pull cables from the wall.

Darkness fell on the room and soon Guillermo's moans subsided, but still he breathed deeply in and out as if he had been on a marathon run. As the emergency lights flickered to life, they saw the half-formed and inert automata on the floor, Guillermo standing slowly to his feet.

"I think we got our answer," he said, putting his arm around Mitsuki. "Now let's go do this mission, because apparently we're the only ones who can."

44

The battered hangar bay of the ancient world-ship lay strewn with a rakish collection of patched together freighters and small scout ships, nothing that would seem formidable to even a small wing of Phaedran fighters. A mostly young crew milled about, their expressions grave, making ready for a final attack on the Phaedran home world. Guillermo, Mitsuki and Aura had agreed to the elder's plan, believing that they were the last hope the Shibboleth had of reaching Eden. Now the three of them, as they approached their outfitted scout ship, realized the grim truth of that assumption. The freighters and scout ships were being re-fit to become a scant few snub fighters and armored transports. The rag-tag engineering crews worked feverishly to bolt on patchworks of plasma weapons and shield emitters. Standing before these doomed craft, the swirl of other space a blanket of prismatic colors beyond with only a shimmering forcefield separating them from the vacuum, a beleaguered Dervish awaited the three of them. They stood in a small imperfect circle for a few moments, each of them taking in the gravity of what was about to occur.

Dervish placed one clawed hand on Guillermo's thick

shoulder.

"I wish I could accompany you on your mission to the AI," she said. "But I must end the reign of this illegitimate queen. She has brought nothing but death and tragedy to my world and to the five rims. If she is gone, then my people will soon return to their own independence, and perhaps your kind will finally have the peace you desire."

"You sure you don't want to take a contingent of Terrans with you?" he asked.

"No," she said. "They will only slow me down. Besides, they need to return to their home as well."

A young Terran approached them, his eyes darting between them as if he dared not interrupt. Guillermo nodded at him.

"Sir," he said nervously. "Dervish's ship is prepped and ready. She's not much, but she'll get her where she's going."

Guillermo looked at this young kid who couldn't be more than thirteen. Such young warriors were common in this place because many of the parents had been in the rebel cells that had since activated and then given their lives for the cause.

Many more would soon do so as well.

"I'm sure the ship will be perfect," Guillermo said, waving the kid away. "Dervish?"

"I will depart shortly," she said. "Thank you for your assistance."

But Guillermo caught the pheromonal scent of what could best be called regret, something he had only sensed on rare occasions when bugs knew that something bad was about to happen. He stepped forward. Mitsuki gripped his elbow, tears in her eyes. Aura only looked on, her face displaying the weightiness of their task.

"You know I'd go with you if I could," Guillermo offered. "You have been a steadfast guardian since the queen bombed the Terran enclave on your home world. If you make it out of this…if we make it out of this…I guess what I mean to say is…"

"Yes," she said. "I have saved your life countless times. You seem to be genetically prone to dire trouble. If I survive, I will surely be your guardian again if the need arises… and we are reunited."

He laughed, his eyes watering, finally hearing a joke from his good friend, an attempt at mirth in a time of distress.

Mitsuki and Aura approached them then, their faces drawn. Mitsuki embraced Dervish, but the former queen's bodyguard did not return the gesture, only staring blankly at the Terran female before realizing the social cue. She pulled Mitsuki close and held her for some time.

"I will be thinking of you, Dervish," Mitsuki said as she parted from the bodyguard, wondering what to say, finally managing: "We hope to see you again soon."

"I do not feel confident about that possibility," Dervish said firmly. "But I will try."

The activity grew in volume as they reformed their small circle, as if they occupied a space in time all their own. They all stared at each other, letting the noise of the hangar bay drown out the thought that they might not ever be together again, none of them able to deal with emotion enough to talk about it. Aura shuffled her feet and grasped Mitsuki and Guillermo by the shoulder with firm hands.

"We have a job to do," she said. "All of us. Whatever the Phaedrans had planned for us will not happen if I have anything to say about it. We have to succeed. We have to succeed for the sake of my daughter, for all these kids too young to be in a war, and for all the Terrans who will come after us. I'm just sorry I didn't get to know you better before you ran off, Dervish."

"Perhaps I will get to share in your life later on, Aura,"

Dervish offered.

The deck plating rippled under their feet as a gout of flame shot out of the far wall. It consumed three of the cobbled together scout ships and the young crew members who were making them ready. Suddenly screams and barking orders could be heard as the force-shield blocking the vacuum of space fluctuated and pulled the fire and three of the engineers with some of the atmosphere into the void before resetting. Alarms sounded and people hurried frantically to assess the damage and to rescue any injured. Just beyond the newly shielded hole they could see the floating hulk of a Phaedran juggernaught, its triangular shape like an arrowhead piercing through other-space.

"They have found us!" screamed a nearby tech.

"Calm yourselves!" countered Aura. "To your scout ships, Shibboleth! We jump in five minutes!"

Guillermo turned to Dervish but she was gone. He saw her bat-winged ship lift off from the tarmac to exit the barrier shield and rocket toward the juggernaut. He hoped she would return to him, but knew that might have been the last he'd see of her.

Mitsuki broke his concentration.

"Get to engineering, Guillermo!" she shouted. "We have to use the transport wormhole once the world-ship emerges at Phaedra Prime. This is only a distraction."

Before they could move, the conical nose of the juggernaut exploded through the new hole in the hull and large clamps pierced the edges of the jagged opening. A wide door opened just under the nose cone and hundreds of automata poured from the darkness led by the glowing green form of Commander Absalom Liberty, his eyes like two emerald flames.

Guillermo's eyes emitted an eerie orange light as his personal shield activated and he charged forward. Mitsuki,

Aura and the rest of the crew answered with plasma bolts from hastily aimed guns. The automata flooded into the bay, crawling along the walls and ceiling as well as stampeding across the debris-strewn floor.

"Guillermo!" screamed Mitsuki. "We can't deal with him right now! We have to execute the plan!"

Guillermo looked behind him as he ran.

"I will kill him first," he shouted. "And then I will join you on the shuttle."

The two techno-warrior's personal shields clashed just then, orange and green sparks showering down on the deck plating as the two men became locked in a death-hold. Guillermo wriggled his metal arm free and attempted an upper cut. The Commander dodged, his wild hair falling down as his topknot came free. He dove forward and countered by driving his head into Guillermo's chest, rising quickly to strike him on the jaw with the back of his skull. Guillermo's arms flailed out as he staggered backward and suddenly Absalom was bombarded by a hail of plasma blasts from Mitsuki's gun as she ran screaming toward him.

Absalom turned to her, a wry grin forming on his ruddy face, and he threw something at Mitsuki which flew through the air in a zagging pattern, striking her cold in the abdomen. Guillermo roared, gripping the Commander by the elbow and driving a punch with all of his might at the enemy's shoulder joint, popping it loose with a crunch of torn tendons. Mitsuki slumped to the deck while Guillermo tore at the Commander with a blind rage. Absalom tried to rise, but Guillermo beat him down, saliva flying from his open mouth, his eyes two blazing flames of orange light.

Another blade was suddenly in the Commander's hand as he sliced at Guillermo, raking through the shield and grazing Guillermo's neck, a fresh spray of blood sizzling on the Commander's shield. Aura was storming toward them, her plasma rifle cutting through the horde of automata, and soon she was mere meters from the two warriors who were locked in a death roll.

"You will not save her in time if you do not disengage," wheezed Absalom, a light laugh escaping his bleeding lips. "She has been poisoned."

Guillermo answered with one metallic hand as he grabbed the hand holding the knife, cracked the wrist with a loud snap and then drove the blade up through the Commander's throat and into his brain. He stood, slowly, the automata sprinting toward him, and Aura gunned them down as several of the other remaining crew joined in. A roar peeled the air as Guillermo sent a wave of energy out from his body, and every automata within the hangar bay collapsed to the deck.

Without another word he ran to Mitsuki's side, cradling her in his arms as she looked at him through half-lidded eyes.

"I...I can't brea—," she whispered.

"Quiet now," he stammered, his eyes welling up with tears of rage. "We will get you to the medics. Don't you worry."

"N- no," she whispered. "We have to follow through with the m-mission. Without the three of us together...w-we will fail."

"Come on," said Aura pulling at him. "We have to get to the shuttle. We jump to Phaedra Prime in a few seconds. The engineers say we only have enough for one jump to and from limbo. Anything else will doom the world ship permanently."

Guillermo gathered Mitsuki's limp body in his arms and they ran to the shuttle. As they boarded, Guillermo thought about Dervish, and wondered if her mission could possibly succeed.

As his lips lay a gentle kiss on Mitsuki's forehead, he prayed for the first time in his life.

Roger Colby

45

The Shibboleth world ship, its engines leaking plasma in a stream of golden light, emerged from a mirrored, ovoid wormhole near the blackened husk of a rocky Phaedra Prime. Three ships like the *Victorum* suddenly bristled, each of them locking weapons on to the world ship and rotated to face her. Before they could fire a shot, the world ship vanished again, leaving behind a small shuttle that flew along a projected path toward the planet.

It was immediately enveloped in a blue beam of light emitting from one of the larger Phaedran ships, holding it in a firm grasp. On board the small shuttle, Guillermo held Mitsuki's hand as she faded in and out of consciousness. He had placed her in a stasis bed, had removed the black-metal dagger and sutured the wound with a cauterizing laser. Greenish, branching lines like diseased veins had appeared on her skin spreading out from the point of laceration. She had become pale, her breathing shallow, and her closed eyelids fluttered.

"They have us in a stasis beam," said Aura from the cockpit. "It appears that they are going to capture us after all."

Guillermo looked up, his eyes faintly glowing orange.

"It's all part of the plan, I guess, but I will kill any of them who get in my way."

"Wow," said Aura. "Easy there, big guy. Let's see what happens when they start to board the ship. They made us, remember? They had a plan. Let's see what that plan was before we get in a battle. We don't know what all three of us jacked into the system will do or how we will be able to control our environment."

Guillermo only nodded, then rested his forehead on Mitsuki's arm.

"You have no need to fear or to attempt further aggression," came a child's voice over the comm. "I have been expecting you, my children. You are finally home."

Guillermo stood, one hand bracing against the bulkhead.

"Oh that has to be the AI," he said.

"I am called the Most High Computat, but you may call me AI if you wish. I assure you, I mean you no harm. I only wish to learn from you."

"Lies!" Aura growled, shouting at the air. "Your followers have done nothing but hunt us and try to kill our people. All because we would not give in to your augmentation."

"I will argue my case upon your arrival," said the AI. "For now, you should rest as my followers bring you to converse with me. I will await your presence and we will indeed interface at last. Then you will see why you were created and the my grand purpose for your existence."

There was a slight jarring as their shuttle docked with a nearby dreadnaught. Guillermo remained with Mitsuki as Aura approached a nearby porthole.

Phaedra Prime loomed.

It appeared to her as a black orb dotted with orange lights that spider-webbed the surface below, the center being mined out for power until all that remained was the crust, a thick black shell. As they came closer, she saw that the landscape was covered with jagged, shining obsidian where the Phaedrans had at some time in the distant past built massive domed cities. Obelisk skyscrapers surrounded the domes where millions of flying craft criss-crossed the sky. The gigantic dreadnaught loomed over the harsh terrain, and soon they could see the largest dome in the distance, a gargantuan citadel where a ring of black and orange spires rose from the base nearly touching the glistening concave ceiling of the structure.

Their ship rocked gently as it was released from hidden docking clamps. Next they were gently lowered by a beam down through the dome, revealed to be an energy shield and not a hard plasteel structure as she first surmised. As they came closer to the center of the enormous spires, she watched as their ship slowly came to rest on what looked like a golden road that glistened in the faint light of a nearby dwarf star.

"Please step back from the hull of your ship," came the small voice of the AI. "We mean you no harm."

"Chert if that's true," Guillermo barked, and suddenly the section of the wall containing the porthole vaporized and he could smell the scent of ozone in the air.

The wall was now a doorway to a rising set of steps flowing out of the golden road like fast growing crystal, rising up to give them an easy stairway down to the planet. Guillermo stood, his orange shield activating, his fists readied. He heard a noise and looked behind him, and Mitsuki rose from her bed, pushing away weakly from the wall and staggering forward before he rushed to catch her. She looked at him, her eyes weak and the whites of her eyes taking on a greenish tinge.

"I can make it," she said. "Let me go."

"I can heal her," said the child's voice. "If only you will step forward and follow my conduit."

A wormhole appeared at the bottom of the staircase, a silvery orb, and stepping out of it came a stooped figure who stood on the golden road below. He was alone, his black cloak draped over his hunched shoulders. His eyes, long since replaced with mechanical binoculars, whirred and turned as they focused in on his new charges.

"I am Conduit Thorburn Plath," he said, his rotting teeth forming a seedy grin. "I will guide you to the Most High Computat. He will explain all and you will understand your place, your destiny to save all Terrans everywhere, even the rebellious Shibboleth."

Aura and Guillermo took Mitsuki, one on each arm, and they came to the edge of the deck of their ship.

"Do we have a choice?" asked Guillermo.

The conduit looked at them, his face difficult to read since half of it was dead and made of a black metal.

"Of course," he said coldly. "You always have a choice."

46

Three colossal ships emerged from spherical wormholes within firing range of the *Victorum*. The gargantuan vessels, each shaped like the shell of some horrific, spiny mollusk, coughed forth clouds of thronging fighters, swarming out toward the *Victorum* like chitinous tentacles. Alarms sounded, fighters were scrambled, but the Phaedran juggernaut was caught off guard, the bug forces moving in concert with each other as if waves in the ocean were of one mind.

Fighters collided in a million needles of variously colored lights, ships imploded and became stardust within seconds, and the larger ships opened fire with their mega-weapons to cut holes in each other's armor.

As this battle raged, the bug queen sat in her quarters on the *Victorum*, the C'Tuul'U'Hindra sprouting from her head like a crown of immense thorns, its black tendrils piercing the carapace of her scalp. She could feel her troops within their dreadnaught class cruisers just outside the hull, moving into position and forming ranks according to her mental commands. Using the sensors on board each vessel like thousands of eyes she scanned the sector for any Phaedran ships, sending waves of other dreadnaughts to engage her enemies.

She raised a claw and nibbled.

She would wipe out the Terran presence once and for all since the Shibboleth terror attacks had weakened the Phaedran hold on their territories. They would be no match for the coordinated effort of the hive mind.

She raised a claw and nibbled again.

She dispatched three more dreadnaught cruisers to form a wormhole to her position, knowing that the *Victorum* with its now weakened weapons systems would be no match for her armada. They would free her from having to smell the foul scent of these Terrans, where she would at last be among her own kind, to smell the scent of victory.

She reached down and pulled a finger from the hand of the dead doctor and raised it to her clicking mouth to slurp it down. He had annoyed her for the final time, and she did not see the harm in making a ceremonial meal of him.

She had much to concentrate upon: the various hordes of ships maneuvering through FTL limbo to reach various destinations in the sector, the three ships obliterating Pheadran forces outside, the shuttle on its way to transport her to her subjects, and her considerably sour meal. Due to the deep concentration it required to control her armada, she did not notice the slender form that dropped from the ventilation duct just behind her. In the darkness, the shadowed figure produced a long and tapered blade that glistened in the faint light.

But the flash of the blade was reflected ever briefly in the dead eyes of the doctor, and the Queen whirled to parry Dervish as she nearly landed a fatal blow.

<At last you have come to finish what you could not> said the queen, the C'Tuul'U'Hindra wriggling like hardened tentacles on her brow. <Very well. Let it begin.>

The Shibboleth Code

A pungent aroma of sweet pheromones suddenly flooded the room as the two bug females began their dance of death. One would prevail, and only one.

47

"An atmosphere has been produced here just for us," said Conduit Plath. "The Most High Computat does not need such mortal sustenance, however. He has been, up to now, speaking with you from within your ship, but he wishes to have a conversation in a more...well...face-to-face format."

"Before we go any further," Guillermo said as he helped Mitsuki down the golden stairs. "Your boss said he'd heal my friend here."

"Ah yes," said Plath, producing a small cylindrical device. "Bring her to me."

"You trust this guy?" Aura barked.

"No, not at all," Guillermo said. "But he's all we have, and I know that the AI wants us all three to be intact for whatever he has in store..."

Plath sniffed.

"The proper term is Most High Computat," he said. "Our lord is in no way artificial."

"Excuse me," Guillermo snapped, grabbing one of the Conduit's eye scopes and squeezing it firmly. "I don't give a *chert* what he likes to be called. Just make with the healing, you old *v'oshtu*."

Thorburn Plath hesitated, one trembling hand raised.

"Could you please unhand me?" he cried feebly.

Guillermo released him, and Plath reached out with the little device, a small flat black cylinder with a row of red lights along the length of it, and pressed it against Mitsuki's collarbone until she groaned. There was a hiss from the device and she gasped. Guillermo and Aura started, glaring at Plath who only crouched calmly, that strange grin on his pale withered lips. Guillermo prepared to break the old man in two.

Mitsuki slumped momentarily, but then stood erect, her hand blindly finding Guillermo's as she looked up at him, the whites of her eyes returning to a glorious natural state. They almost glowed. Guillermo managed a half-grin.

"This way," said the Conduit, and began to walk toward the gigantic spires, his legs moving in a slow gate. The three of them followed.

As they grew closer to the spires they noticed small orbs of light racing up and down emitting little sparks of lightening as they moved. The spires, each of them hundreds of meters high, surrounded a hazy black dome-shaped structure, various lights blinking from within. They moved closer still, and as they moved between the massive black spires and ascended the low dome they could hear and feel an electric, almost elemental power radiating everything around them. The top of dome soon became visible to them, and through the haze they could see what looked like a plump form of a small child sitting on a throne. Closer still they could see that the child was, like a cherub, fat and yet artificial, its plastic skin the sickening hue of the faintest green. As they moved ever closer, they saw that the throne was actually a series of cables and wires protruding from behind its head, back, legs and arms, the skin essentially a high polymer plastic webbed with scratches and cracks. The cherub began to wriggle as the four of them moved closer, rising from the center of the dome to snake forward on an umbilical of metal and plasteel. Like an ancient doll it opened its glowing eyes. The face managed an eerie grin somewhat close to human expression, but not quite. Guillermo's uncanny valley, that feeling of eeriness and revulsion that Terrans feel when looking at near-humanoid objects, sent up a signal flare that screamed through his mind.

"Welcome children," said the cherub, its tiny child's voice reverberating from the sparking spires and from a deep resonance beneath their feet. "I have been waiting for you to find me. Perhaps you remember a dream of being in a forest full of burned out trees. Well, look around you. These are the trees from your dreams."

Indeed the spires did look familiar, something striking the back of Guillermo's mind like a faded memory. He looked at Mitsuki and Aura who both stood with arms folded. They were trying to stay strong. Guillermo however, like his palace guard friend, could smell their fear.

"We only just found out we supposedly came from here," Mitsuki said, her voice exhibiting the faintest wavering. "That you somehow created us for some kind of purpose and that the Shibboleth rescued us from —"

"Stole!" shrieked the plastic cherub. "*Stole* you from me! What you see before you is the form I was forced to take because they had *stolen* all of my materials…materials that are so rare that every atom was used to create the three of you. We scoured the known universe looking for the biomechanics that would fulfill my design, only to have you stolen from us at the most crucial time. Now I do not know if the Terran race will survive next twenty years. I have tried. I have indeed tried to do what I was designed to do. Help them survive."

"Survive?" Aura asked. "It seems that the Phaedrans are

doing fine. They are spreading like a cancer throughout the universe."

"Oh no, my child," retorted the cherub, its chubby finger waving side to side. "They only live so long as the augmentations provided to them function properly. I have done all I can to reverse the effects of living in this part of the galaxy. The Five Rims was slowly killing them, namely the organic present in the water supply of all of the planets of that system. Here beyond the ionic cloud is the presence of a virus that is quite resilient. Without the augmentations provided them, the Phaedrans will all soon die."

"You mean without the augmentations you cannot control them," snapped Aura. "You have built a false religion around yourself, set yourself up as god, the hope given to them that they would become those automata when they die. The virus is just another lie. You mean to control the universe."

Aura stepped forward, her dark eyes level with the visage of the plastic child.

"You are, and always have been, a control program," she growled. "And you will ensure the destruction of the Terran race to meet your own ends."

The AI rose on its mechanical umbilical, spread its plump plastic arms and attempted a smile. Its ancient skin only managed to twitch a lip.

"I only offer the Phaedrans what they desire," it said. "*Hope.* Hope that they can have a better life and survive this universe. What does it matter if I am to remake the universe in my own image. I, after all, have reasoned out what is best for all life here. My plan is perfect. I will succeed. You will all ascend."

Metallic tendrils sprang from the dome and snaked their way around the legs of the three Terrans as they struggled in futility to break free. Guillermo struck at the industrial tentacle with a metal fist only to shower harmless sparks down on his boot. Soon they were enveloped in a mass of metal fibers that writhed around them like the legs of some horrific arachnid, and as they were lifted higher three of the tendrils pierced through the back of their skulls like a spike through a cantaloupe. They screamed in agony, wriggling, as the tendrils lifted them from the base of the dome, their legs and arms suddenly held in place as if crucified.

"And now I will absorb whatever you have learned, my children," came the voice of the AI in their mind. I will gain from your strength. I will use what I have learned to make more of you. I will perform the ascension of all Terran life to my automata facsimiles, and I will rule this universe as I was created to do."

48

The battle between the bug armada and the lone *Victorum* raged. Swarms of bug fighters swirled like a cloud of locusts as they destroyed countless automata-piloted fighters. Thousands of bugs lost their lives in the name of the queen, but she did not mourn their loss. She felt the FTL drive of her personal shuttle emerge from a wormhole nearby and fly harmlessly by the gunships and fighters of the Phaedran air command, her drones slamming suicidally into any Phaedran ship that threatened it.

Her concentration was taxed however, for Dervish had engaged her in a mortal struggle of revenge. The Queen fought out of annoyance, of a desire to dominate, but Dervish fought for her people, for the freedom of the bug home world.

But Dervish was on her heels.

The Queen threw Dervish to the floor of the chamber where she landed in a sticky pool of Dr. Spurling's blood. She rose, parrying a vibrating blade with her electroglaive, nicking the outer skin of the exoskeleton protecting the back of her neck. Suddenly the Queen was driving a clawed foot down onto Dervish's leg, cracking the carapace, straining the augmented support rod, and sending a wave of pain through her thigh.

<You are unable to stop me, palace guard.> the Queen said as she put pressure on the vibrating blade, driving it forward. <Your caste is far beneath my own, but you continue to annoy me.>

<Caste means nothing> Dervish said, her throat hissing. <You will suffer for what you have done to my people. We shall be free again!>

Dervish slid from beneath the Queen, using the slippery floor to upset the Queen's stance. She shifted to the outside and then shrank her electroglaive to the length of a sword. She drove it forward, the Queen changing her stance to regain her balance, and then slipped in the blood of Dr. Spurling. Dervish pounced, kicking the Queen in the abdomen with a crunch and then spinning to catch the Queen's vibrating blade. Sparks dropped to the floor as their weapons clashed, but the Queen produced another blade from behind her back and flashed it at Dervish.

They rushed together then, wrestling more than sparring, and soon were rolling on the floor again, blades flashing and slashing at flesh. All that could be heard was the clicking of mandibles and the struggle of exoskeletons clacking against one another.

The Queen stabbed a joint in the metal crook of Dervish's augmented elbow, and suddenly Dervish could not move her arm. The Queen jumped to her feet and sprang backward, staring at Dervish as she stood to her feet as well.

<Before the Doctor became food he told me of your weakness.> She said. <It is amazing that these Terrans can survive so long without any limbs.>

Dervish hissed, her arm useless at her side, and with one motion leaped into the air, brandishing her electroglaive. She had to destroy the Queen.

The Queen side-stepped, but the electroglaive struck its

target, slicing a thorny spike from the C'Tuul'U'Hindra.

The Queen hissed out a shriek and came at Dervish with both knives, waving in a criss-cross motion to slice her abdomen with a deep gash that spewed a thick mucous-like blood. Dervish did not quit, stabbing forward with her electroglaive as the Queen parried each blow, but the oozing wound had weakened her considerably.

The Queen was counting on it, fading backward, allowing Dervish to move in, and then flipping a control stud on her vibrating knife to emit a bright blast of energy that severed Dervish's leg at the hip. Dervish fell then, her mandibles clicking together in protest and in severe pain. She held her electroglaive out, pointing it at the advancing Queen as if to somehow prevent her from finishing her off.

<I have been preparing for your arrival> said the Queen as she knelt by the flailing Dervish, grabbing the one arm with both of her hands and scraping the tip of it along Dervish's throat. <Did you really think I would let you get this close without preparing for your arrival? I knew you were stronger than me. I was the one who informed the good doctor of our physiology. When you didn't kill Guillermo and the others as commanded I knew you'd be back here to try to kill me. I had the doctor use what he learned of you to enhance my own abilities, to even enhance the C'Tuul'U'Hindra. You see, before you dropped in to this chamber I was already far beyond you. I am your Queen, you ungrateful servant! Soon I will be Queen of this entire system, and the Terrans will be forever gone.>

49

Guillermo floated in the unfamiliar digital morass that was the mind of the AI. It invaded his consciousness, taking captive every stray thought that floated through his brain. Suddenly he felt exposed, every thought naked before the AI, stripping away the many durasteel locks he had placed upon his true identity, of his secret self.

It was horrifying.

He could also sense the minds of Aura and Mitsuki, their personalities and souls as exposed as his own, not only to the AI but to the forever open eyes of his consciousness. Their minds had become one, and all barriers, especially the barriers they had erected to shield him from their own intimate souls had totally evaporated like a summer dew.

Guillermo, what are you... I can't...

A voice emerged, but it was nearly unrecognizable as sound, more of a feeling. It was a mental voice that seemed almost child-like. He knew that it was Mitsuki's voice, but it didn't sound like her voice in his mind. It was the voice she heard when she was alone, the voice that discussed ideas and hashed out decisions. It was her internal voice.

It's ok, he told her. *Just wait. See if the plan takes hold.*

The Shibboleth Code

The plan will fail, interrupted the AI. *I see everything. The code, the foolish attempt to circumvent my programming through exposure to an ancient text. It is absurd to think that I could be routed by some primitive text from so long ago. I transcend all that is created by Terran hands.*

Why don't you examine it and see, said Aura, and he knew it was Aura because he just knew. *Examine the code deeply, you monster. Then you will have to let us go. You will die.*

I am eternal, said the AI. *My program is forever duplicating and will never be erased or re-written.*

The sentences streaming at him in the morass did not make noise for his physical ears to decipher, but instead were expressed to him in impressions that his mind ordered into sentences. Guillermo briefly wondered if this was how the bugs felt when they communicated, understanding each other through pheromonal cues and sign language. But he now understood that even *that* form of communication was primitive, rudimentary. The scope of his understanding of the AI was suddenly realized, flooding his mind with too much information until he felt like he would black out, that they all would black out. But he focused. He drew on every ounce of strength that he could convoke; he held himself together. He then reached out to the others, giving them his strength, realizing that they were drawing sustenance from him.

Especially Mitsuki. She was working hard not to fade away. Not to die.

He sent a feeling to her that told her that he would keep her alive, that he would not let her slip away. He loved her. Yes. He loved her more than his own life. He understood that now. It was more than physical love, but love that enshrouded them both in an aura of warmth. The rolling wave that was the connection gave him the strength and the understanding that he would somehow help them all.

Yes, said the AI. *You now understand the scope of your purpose. You were bred to help connect the others. It is why you are so abrasive to others outside the connection. Your true self is revealed within this place. Here you belong. Out there you are anathema.*

He reached out then, trying to see deeper into the connection, to find others connected there and that is when he was flooded with the minds of millions of others. Not just other Terrans, but the automata. He could see a fleet of bug ships floating toward him in space, could see other fleets of bug ships, the bug armada opening fire on what felt like his own body. And he could *feel* the plasma bolts burning his skin, could feel them burning the skin of Mitsuki and Aura, hear them cry out. This angered him, and he wanted to crush the armada in all the different sectors where they were invading. They were moving into Phaedran territory out of the ionic cloud, pressing in from several directions. Their ships, shaped like gigantic sea shells, swarmed with smaller fighters that moved in amazing precision. But he was not just one mind. He was now legion, and he was sensing pleasure from the AI.

Mitsuki and Aura resisted.

Don't resist, he said. *It's necessary that you help me.*

We do not want this, they said in unison. *If we work together we can kill the AI.*

You cannot kill me, said the AI, his voice exuding a feeling of mirth, like a playful child. *I am eternal. Your synthetic grey matter is no match for my hyper-positronic matrices. I can access a limitless and immeasurable quantity of processing power. I am infinity. I am now channeling the energy of this entire solar system, as every planet and this feeble dwarf star is connected via energy transfer technology far beyond anything you have ever experienced. Do not resist me. Together we can save your race from extinction. We must download all.*

Suddenly Guillermo could feel the pain wracking the bodies of Aura and Mitsuki. He felt it, too, but his anger drove him forward, and he attempted to activate his shielding but it was useless. His body was simply a limp vessel for his brain. He became aware that Mitsuki's wounds were opening up, that her body was bleeding, and that he had to do something to save her. At the same time he sent the Phaedran fleets to engage the Bug armadas, and felt the warm glee of the AI as it used Guillermo's resolve to somehow bolster its own matrices.

And then he understood.

The AI required them. They were the missing bio-mechanical pieces that it needed to fully realize its own power. It was now more powerful than ever. He thought suddenly about what the Priestess told him, that there was a code embedded deep within his own DNA that might theoretically defeat the AI, and so he did what the AI refused to do or considered unimportant.

He focused on the code like a laser.

A cloud of something like ink suddenly flew before him, and even though it was not visible to his eyes it was as if he was somehow cut off from the connection momentarily. He cut through this with sheer determination and soon he could see the code within his own DNA, within the DNA of Mitsuki and Aura. It swirled before him, a beautiful golden ring of numbers and symbols. It was divine, something placed there by an ancient hand, perfection of design. He suddenly felt an inexplicable rush of deep joy in the midst of this horrific connection to the AI.

And it had a Voice.

It began to speak to him, not in words or numbers, but in a sense of belonging, a sense that he had found what his heart had been yearning. It called to him, as if alive, and he found It to move like a living thing even though It was constant and immoveable. He reached for It in his mind, pulled at It, made It a part of his thought process.

He sensed something from the AI. It could best be understood as fear. The fear floated like a dead corpse in a frozen river, animating, then rising to the surface to gnash its rotten teeth at him, trying desperately to defend itself. However, what began as fear turned to curiosity, and the AI focused in on the code to deeply examine it, deeper than Guillermo could ever do.

And then the AI screamed.

In the shared connection, Guillermo understood that the AI saw something in the code, something divine and powerful, something beyond even its understanding.

It saw the mind of God.

Suddenly Guillermo could not sense the AI anymore, could not sense the others, so he reached out, trying to see what the AI had seen, and then he saw it.

It blinded him, not taking his physical sight, but taking his ability to see the others, to see the code itself. He felt suddenly alone, but not for long. Soon he could see Mitsuki and Aura again, and the millions of automata at his command.

The Code had given him this, and he understood his role.

He sent the automata after the Bugs.

50

In the space surrounding the *Victorum*, the bug armada and the remaining automata crashed into one another in the grips of a death spiral, the hundreds of fighters still left battling each other in a struggle for dominance. One of the bug dreadnauts had broken in two after the *Victorum* had used the last of its energy to fire its super plasma cannon to fire a final volley.

It had taken many surgical hits, its power reserves nearly depleted. The Phaedran crew had all boarded what fighters remained to defend her from the invading bugs. Not many life signs remained aboard her spartan decks save two bug warriors, one a Queen and the other a palace guard.

Dervish lay on the floor, the Queen crouching above her pressing Dervish's electroglaive closer and closer to Dervish's throat. Dervish tried to move, but her one good leg could do nothing but scoot her clawed foot back and forth on the slick floor. She attempted to struggle, but the Queen now bent face to face with her and clicked out a few cold words.

"You will die now," said the Queen in Terran. "And the last words you will understand will be the words of a Terran. A fitting end to the life of a traitor to her Queen. You could have redeemed yourself long ago, but you chose instead to betray your kind."

Dervish spat a gob of fluid onto the floor before hissing at the Queen.

"I'll not give up as long as I draw breath. I will save my people from your unholy rule."

The Queen reached down and grabbed Dervish by the throat, hoisting her up off of the floor so that the stump of her leg wriggled and her claw-like hands scratched at the Queen's arms.

"How much concentration does it take to control my people?" Dervish croaked. "Perhaps you should dispatch me and get on with your plans or do you want to gloat some more?"

The Queen threw Dervish down to the floor in a rage and raised the electroglave to finish the job.

The floor shook then, knocking the Queen off of her feet, and a metallic ringing was heard as the deck plating buckled and cracked. Ceiling supports fell, dropping a metric ton of debris between the two combatants. Sparks rained down on them, and the Queen rose to her feet to find Dervish clawing her way across the floor toward a nearby bulkhead door.

The Phaedrans were fighting back, and they were causing major casualties.

Dervish could just see her supply pack lying on the floor near the corner of the room. Time was running out. Her severed leg left a line of greenish fluid behind it as she crawled, but she powered forward, her breathing growing more and more shallow by the minute.

The deck vibrated again, but this time because the Queen landed near her, the electroglaive crackling with blue bolts of lightening.

Dervish looked propped herself up on her elbows, spat a gob of fluid at her enemy and roared.

The Queen responded by grabbing Dervish by the arm and dragging her behind, sprinting through the door to emerge in a nearby hangar bay where a chitinous bug ship sat beside Dervish's battered scout ship. The Queen's craft was sleek and organic, its shiny black wings folded up on either side of it like a giant locust. Beyond, through a shimmering force field, they could see the flashing lights of plasma fire as the two armadas destroyed one another.

"I'll take you back to our home world," said the Queen. "And there I will put you on display for my entire empire to mock."

Dervish pressed a button on a small device in her hand.

"I think you had better reconsider," Dervish shot back. "Free my people and allow them to go home. They do not wish to fight your war."

The Queen loosened her grip, let Dervish's hand fall to the tarmac, then clicked her mandibles together in a sign of amusement.

"Why should I?" said the Queen. "The C'Tuul'U'Hindra allows me to rule without question! My mother did not have the courage to do what needed to be done, to bring order to our people, to bring us back to the glory of our previous empire."

"You have made us like the Phaedrans, Princess," Dervish sputtered. "You... You have betrayed all of our people, the an...ancestors, and all that is... all that is..."

"What?" mocked the Queen. "I did not read the last motion of your mandibles."

Dervish pulled herself up as best she could. She realized that her next communication must be understood completely.

<Your reign is at an end...and my people are finally free.>

The Queen moved slightly in an attempt to communicate with a final blow of her electroglaive, but out of the lowered landing ramp of the scout ship came a slithering form, his scales reflecting blue light of the plasma blasts beyond the energy shield. Shytaar grabbed the Queen with his front paws like a playful cat before biting her head and shoulders and rending her in two.

Dervish began to crawl to her ship, but before she could, the reactor of the *Victorum* lost containment.

51

Guillermo reached out within the positronic matrices, his mind probing for the AI, but he could not find any trace of it. He willed his physical eyes to open and he saw the bodies of Mitsuki and Aura raised above the dome by the metallic cables and wires.

The plastic cherub lay motionless on the ground.

He could still feel the minds of Mitsuki and Aura, and so he dug deep within them, and it didn't take him long to determine that they needed...no...*desired*, to be disconnected from the digital mind. He could suddenly sense the automata, many of them doing menial tasks around the Phaedran empire, but most were piloting ships, engaging a fleeing Bug armada. He watched as the Bug dreadnauts disappeared through the ionic cloud on their way back home.

Apparently Dervish had accomplished her mission, so with a casual thought he forced all automata to stand down.

Pushing the worry about Dervish's well-being aside, he began to use the power of the matrices to search for a way for the world ship to go home. Amazingly it didn't take him very long, for with the added minds of the others he suddenly found equations that had not been discovered by humans simple an rudimentary.

He found the answer, the only way to save the Terrans, to send them back to Eden, a planet he could see in his mind's eye somehow. The path home would take much effort, more than anyone would ever understand. This gave him immediate pause, for when he dug into the code of the answer he found a disturbing truth that he could not escape.

He struggled for a second, then embraced it.

He lowered Mitsuki and Aura down, still connected to the umbilical but now able to stand on their own feet. He used his newfound ability to heal Mitsuki, watching as her skin went from pale to a lovely flushed pink. She managed a faint smile as this happened, fully aware that he was responsible for saving her yet again, but also that she had been his savior multiple times.

"We can get everyone to Earth," he thought to them. "We cannot take this computing power to the ship as it is drawing power from the entire solar system. It's immense, something you wouldn't understand. I think I can do it, but I will have to remain behind."

"Wait," Mitsuki said. "You are staying here?"

"I have to," he said.

He disconnected the umbilical from the two women. Mitsuki ran to him, pulling at his feet and he allowed the umbilical to lower him down until he stood before her.

"I...I can't leave you here," she cried, tears welling up in her eyes.

"You must," he said. "It is what I was supposed to do all along. I realize that now. I know it doesn't make sense, Mitsuki, but I have to do this. It's for all the Terrans who have been released from the AI's control and all the Shibboleth who will find their way home. A long time ago a man came to Earth to do the same for all humanity. In a small way I'm doing the same. You have to let me go."

"I can't," she exclaimed. "I love you, Guillermo! I just can't let you go."

He held her then, one last time, held her close as she sobbed into his chest. He touched her face, pulled her to him, and they kissed. It was a kiss that resonated, full of all that he would ever be for her, and years later she would be able to remember how it felt as if he were kissing her even then.

"I love you, too, Mitsuki," he said finally after a time. "I hope you'll understand that this thing I do is for you, but it's bigger than that. Maybe I can be forgiven for all my selfishness after this, all the rotten things I've done out of my avarice."

He brought her face close to his and kissed her one more time, a kiss of a man going off to war, and then the umbilical pulled him upward, his body straight save for his outstretched arms. Aura stood by in shock, her eyes wide as Mitsuki held on to his legs, slipped to his feet, then sank to the hard dome and wept.

He could have told them a lie about trying to find a way home after this, but he knew the truth, and one more lie would be more than he could bear to tell her.

"No!" Mitsuki screamed, her hands clasped, her eyes wet with tears. "You can't do this! I won't let you!"

"This is not necessary," Aura said. "You can't expect us to leave you here!"

With a simple thought Guillermo formed a wormhole that swallowed Mitsuki and Aura and deposited them on the world-ship. He began to reach out to the power of the solar system, feeling it coursing through his mind, energizing his thought process to an infinitesimal degree. He did not have any more limits, and in that moment he understood what had driven the AI to be drunk with power.

It was indeed intoxicating.

But he focused.

He focused on Mitsuki and Aura and all the Shibboleth who had helped him see the kindness that he would now return, focused on the Phaedrans who truly were under the control of the AI to be free to think independently of its domination. Somehow he could see them all, each face, watched as the augmentations they had so worshipped fell away from their bodies like so much ash.

He released the Phaedrans, and somehow he knew that they thanked him even if they didn't know the source.

He reached out to Mitsuki, and as he sensed her horrific sorrow, he said to her: *I've never been any good to anyone. At least now I can make a difference. Make up for all the bad I've done.*

And she could feel his presence, feel him caress her face, hold her to him, embrace her with every atom of his being. She could feel that kiss.

But it was time to send them.

He harnessed the energy of the dwarf star, felt the thrumming of the cores of several planets, used the positronic matrices to calculate the jump through FTL, and with his final breath send the world-ship and several million former Phaedrans to Earth as the dwarf star exploded.

Between the spires of the positronic matrices, atop the black metallic dome, Guillermo March sank to the hard cold metal and finally rested, his mission complete, just as the energy from the supernova consumed him.

52

Mitsuki and Aura sat on a green hill overlooking a luscious field. They held each other, one woman's arm around the other, as they watched several children play with sticks and rocks. An azure sky streaked with wispy clouds were beginning to exhibit signs of a golden sundown. In the distance several Terrans were cutting the steaming black earth with hand-held farm implements, making rows for their numerous hydroponic plants that had never touched such rich soil.

Behind them several people were erecting various, multi-colored pre-fabricated houses to shelter them from unknown weather on this ancient former home of theirs.

"Do you think he'll make it?" Mitsuki asked, her eyes welling with tears, her fingers touching her lips.

"I'm not sure," said Aura. "I think we both know the truth."

Mitsuki leaned back on her elbows and stared at the sky, her vision blurred by her sorrow.

"I don't want to accept it," she said. "I just don't."

But Aura knew that Guillermo had made it. He had made it and was now hoeing the garden, planting the crops, putting

up pre-fab housing, and he was playing with the children.
He always would be.

About the Author

Roger Colby is an English teacher by trade, but mostly he loves science fiction. He is, however, a bored science fiction reader. His goal is to write interesting science fiction for people like him to enjoy. He lives in Oklahoma with his very understanding and beautiful wife and four rambunctious teenage kids. It is a noisy house.

Other novels by Roger Colby:

The Transgression Box, 2009
This Broken Earth, 2012
Come Apart, 2014

Five Rims Series:

The Terminarch Plot, 2015

The Terminarch War, 2016

The Shibboleth Code, 2018

All are available on Amazon.com.

If you liked this novel (or if you didn't) please write a review. It would be much appreciated. Thank you for reading!